MURDER BY TWILIGHT

BLYTHE BAKER

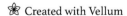 Created with Vellum

~

When Alice Beckingham answers an urgent summons to her sister's home in Yorkshire, she has no idea what dangers are in store for her. From the moment she crosses the threshold, she is enveloped in the same sinister shadows that seem to lie like a mist over the surrounding moorlands.

Determined to discover who is behind an attempt on her sister's life, Alice soon finds herself doubting everyone around her, even her most reliable allies. Without her clever cousin Rose or the protective Sherborne Sharp on hand, can Alice put together the pieces of the haunting puzzle in time to save those dearest to her?

~

1

S hivering, I pulled my coat around my ears and tucked my hands inside the deep pockets, my suitcase wedged between my feet.

Wind whipped through the train platform, seemingly gaining speed as it went, and I felt ill-prepared. I was accustomed to a far-reached cityscape blocking the harshest winds, but Batley in West Yorkshire could not even be compared in size to London, and the wintry winds sliced through the town and my stockings. I shivered and hoped my ride would arrive soon. I was anxious to see my sister.

> *Alice. Come to Yorkshire immediately. Speak to no one. The matter is urgent.*

Catherine's telegram was tucked into my case, and I did not need to pull it out and read it to know what it said. I'd read it countless times on the ship, to the point of memorization. I couldn't get the words out of my mind, and I could not push aside the fear that something sinister was happening at my sister's home.

Aunt Sarah had been disappointed to see me leave New York so soon after arriving, but she understood I needed to be there for Catherine, whatever she was going through. I packed my things and asked a member of Aunt Sarah's staff to send a return telegram, assuring Catherine I would be there as soon as I could. I left on a ship the next day.

Aunt Sarah's position had helped me acquire a last-minute ticket and a private cabin where I spent most of the journey. Enduring polite conversation with the other passengers on board and sitting through stuffy dinners left me jittery and unfocused. I couldn't pretend things were normal and as they always had been because I did not know that for certain. After losing one sibling, the fear that it could happen again gripped me. Whatever was troubling my sister, she was in distress, and I wanted to be with her as soon as I could.

Catherine had instructed me to say nothing to anyone, but failing to tell my plans to our mother and father once I arrived back in London would have caused them alarm. So, I paid them a brief visit, staying only one night, before making an excuse for setting out on another journey.

"You'll make yourself ill with all this travel," Mama had said. "Please, Alice. Stay. We will all journey together to visit Catherine and the baby in a week or two."

"I cannot be away from town right now," Papa argued. He waved me on. "Do as you wish, Alice. One day, all of this travel will tire you, but right now, you are young. Enjoy it."

Mama was angry with Papa the rest of the evening for not forcing me to stay, but still, they both escorted me to the train station the next morning and saw me off with hugs, smiles, and a promise to kiss their new grand-daughter for them.

As I'd boarded the train, I had turned and studied the crowd for any sign of Sherborne Sharp, though I didn't understand why I bothered. There was no way he could have known I was in town, and even if he did, he wouldn't have come to visit me. After reading his rather revealing letter, I'd received Catherine's telegram and forgotten to respond to him. Truly, I hadn't thought of his letter again until the ship made port in London.

Once I'd explained my plans to my parents and been cleared to head immediately to Yorkshire, I excused myself to rest and rushed off to my room where I scribbled out a hasty response.

Sherborne,

First, you'll be pleased to know The Chess Master has been dealt with and disposed of. Just as you did not apologize for warning me to stay away from him, I will not apologize for going after him without your approval. Yes, the mission was dangerous, but it did a great deal of good for a great many people. I have no regrets.

Second, you'll also be pleased to know...I missed you too.

Your friendship is important to me, and I hope I haven't put it in danger by staying silent for several weeks. Something came up and my attention was pulled elsewhere.

I hope to make your life more interesting again soon.

Yours,
     Alice

By the time my letter was likely delivered, the train had departed for Batley in Yorkshire, and I was gone on another adventure.

I hoped I would hear from Sherborne again soon.

I would not leave Yorkshire until I felt certain Catherine and her family were safe, but I couldn't help but hope everything would be resolved quickly; to hope that Catherine's letter had been more dramatic than the situation called for, and I would be on my way back to London shortly. Because although I'd assured my mother I was not weary in the slightest, so many weeks of nonstop travel, excitement, and anxiety had worn on me.

Before I even arrived in London, my brother-in-law Charles had sent word to my parents' home that he would pick me up at the station. Catherine would no doubt be busy at home with the baby, and as eager as I was to see her, I wouldn't dream of asking her to bring my niece to the station just to pick me up. Though, I did wonder how much Charles knew of Catherine's troubles. Had she informed anyone but me that something was wrong? What would he think was the reason for my visit?

Catherine had sent me a telegram despite knowing it would take me a few weeks, at best, to get to her, so what kind of emergency could it really be if several weeks was enough time for me to respond?

I sought to downplay the serious tone of the message, but then I remembered the way Charles and Catherine had both been waiting at the station the last time we had visited. Catherine told us they'd been there for half an hour, awaiting us eagerly. So, why was Charles not already here? Especially since the train had been delayed twenty minutes.

Had something happened to hold him up?

Was I too late to save my sister from whatever trouble had caused her to write?

The thought hit me like a blow to the chest, and I took a deep breath and set my shoulders.

No, everything would be fine. If something terrible was set to happen before my arrival, Catherine would have informed Charles or someone else who could have helped. Everything was all right.

I clung to this thought even as minutes passed by without any sign of Charles.

The railway station in Batley was rather large, with several lines that once connected passengers to other railway stations throughout West Yorkshire. However, those lines had ceased operation as an economy measure during the war a decade ago and were now vacant.

Soon after settling in Yorkshire, Catherine had written about how grateful she was for Charles' employment. It was never something she'd considered before— nor I, given our family's financial blessings throughout our lives—but in Yorkshire, many of the coal and textile mills had closed, leaving people without a job or wages. Though Catherine and Charles lived a comfortable life, according to the letters we'd received, many of their neighbors did not.

I felt as though I could sense that desperation in the station. The unswept floors and the whistling of the wind through the empty platform made it feel abandoned, and

I was eager to be around people again. Preferably my family.

I sat on a bench closest to the road, watching as cars drove past the station, kicking up whirls of dirt. Finally, forty minutes after my train's scheduled arrival time, a car pulled up to the curb, and a rumpled Charles Cresswell climbed out of the driver's seat.

I grabbed my case and hurried towards the car, analyzing his appearance for any sign of distress.

He smiled as I neared him, but I could see the dark circles beneath his eyes and the new wrinkles adorning his face. He looked wan and exhausted as he walked around the car and reached out a hand for my suitcase.

I set the case on the ground before I reached him and wrapped my arms around his middle, surprised by my relief at seeing him.

My brother-in-law had always been a reserved man, very unlike Catherine. He was kind, but not overtly so, and he never showed any special interest in forming a close relationship with me.

Still, the fact that he was alive and seemingly well allowed me to take my first full breath in weeks.

Reluctantly, Charles placed one arm around me and then, slowly, another. Finally, he patted my back with his palm, and I felt him exhale, the breath rustling my hair.

"Thank God you've arrived, Alice."

2

Charles drove the car confidently through the small town, past the town hall with its stone pillars holding up a central pediment. It struck me as rather fanciful compared with the rest of the town. Though, it wasn't the only thing that seemed out of place.

Charles, too, looked strange against his rural backdrop.

He wore the fine clothes similar to what he'd worn when I first saw him in New York City years before, yet, he did not have a driver. He'd picked me up from the train station himself and drove the car confidently as though used to doing so. When I looked closer, I could see the loose threads around his seams and the slight fading in his clothes, and I realized for the first time that Charles and Catherine may not have been as comfortable as they claimed.

Catherine had assured us over and over again that she and Charles were unaffected by the financial troubles the rest of their neighbors faced, but I wondered how true that really was.

"Thank you for picking me up," I said, trying to work out how to bring up the topic of his home's staff without being rude.

"We let our driver go some time back," he said plainly, looking over at me from the corner of his eyes. "I work from the house more often than not, and there aren't many reasons for Catherine to leave home these days, so it seemed an unnecessary expense."

"That is sound reasoning."

I folded my hands in my lap, trying to warm up my chilled fingers. When we were children, Catherine had talked about how fabulously wealthy her future husband would be. While my dreams didn't extend beyond being included in adult after supper conversation, Catherine had big plans that involved a sprawling home with mani-cured lawns, an important spouse who was well-respected in social circles, and beautiful gowns that would send her peers into stunned silences.

Now, she did not even have a driver.

I did not judge them for this, but part of me wondered what Catherine thought about it. Mama had taught us that love could cover a multitude of sins—not to mean lacking money was a sin. Only that love allowed one to see things in a different light. So, under which lighting was Catherine viewing her life now?

We left the town proper and the road became bumpier, giving way to country roads and terrain. Charles did his best to follow the time-worn tracks, but the car still jostled horribly. My case was sliding around in the backseat until it finally fell to the floorboards and became wedged under my seat. Seeking shelter, no doubt.

The landscape dipped and rose all around us, carpets of heather clinging to the last remnants of their purple color before the winter could strip it away fully. Some had already turned full green, still lovely in the way they contrasted with the pale-yellow wild grasses. It was nothing like the well-manicured nature I was accustomed to in the city.

"Catherine wanted to come with me, but we all thought it would be best for her to stay home," Charles said.

"I understand. These roads would be hard on poor little Hazel."

"Yes, Hazel," Charles said, as though the baby had been an afterthought. "That, too."

I frowned. "What other reason would there be? Is Catherine not well enough to manage a short ride into town?"

Charles pressed his lips together like he'd said something he shouldn't have, his forehead wrinkled in concern. Then, his face smoothed out, and he shook his head. "She is physically well."

I didn't like the way he specified which part of her was well. If Catherine truly was fine, he would have said so. But specifying meant some part of my sister was not well at all.

"Charles?" I turned towards him, not bothering to hide my concern. He'd looked so relieved to see me standing along the curb back at the station.

Thank God you've arrived, Alice.

Why? What was going on?

"You know my sister sent me a telegram?" I asked.

Charles nodded. "I oversaw it."

The crease between my brows deepened. "Oversaw it? What does that mean?"

"Catherine has been...confused." Charles turned from a wide dirt road onto another one that was much narrower. The road was smaller but easier to maneuver down because rather than a multitude of tracks, there were very obvious tire marks in the center of the road. It was their driveway.

I'd been so excited to see my sister for so many weeks that it took me by surprise when my heart leapt in my chest.

Nerves gripped my stomach, twisting it into a knot, and I laid a hand down the front of my blouse to try and settle myself. I should have eaten something on the train, but I wasn't hungry, and now I realized why. My appetite had been waning over the last few weeks because I was anxious to arrive at my sister's home and learn the full truth of her troubles. And now, with Charles behaving strangely and evasively, my fear grew.

"Speak plainly, Charles. What is wrong with my sister?"

Charles sat up tall, chin lifted proudly. But the posture only lasted a second before he couldn't bear it any longer. His back slumped forward, his head hanging between his shoulder blades, heavy and dejected. My brother-in-law shook his head and sighed. "I don't know, Alice."

He gripped the steering wheel, flexing his hands against the leather. "I wish I knew. I've tried to uncover what is ailing her, but there seems to be no explanation. It all started with the birth, really."

"The birth?" I gasped. "That was months ago, Charles."

"Really, it started even before that. While she was still pregnant."

My hands shook in my lap, and I folded my fingers together to still them. "What started?"

The house came into view on the hill ahead. My previous visits to my sister's new home had been so brief that I had never paid much attention to my surroundings, but now, as I waited for Charles to choose his words, I noticed the little details before my eyes. It was a long, two-story home with a flat front and square windows. Ivy grew up the front face, but the leaves were sparse, and the vines looked more like grey webs, slowly enveloping the house. I wondered that no groundsman had cut them down but perhaps Charles and Catherine couldn't afford to employ anyone to tend the outside of the property. The house would certainly look more approachable if the grounds were better kept.

A fine mist obscured the top of the house, and the birch trees in the distance had lost many of their leaves. The white trunks stuck from the ground like bones.

"Hallucinations," Charles finally answered my question, as he pulled the car to a stop. He released the wheel slowly and turned to me, his face ashen and nearly the same dirty white color as the plaster finish on his home. "Catherine sees things no one else does, and she talks about spirits and ghosts. I don't know what to do."

Of all the things I'd imagined could be wrong with

my sister, not once had I imagined the trouble would be her mind.

Catherine had always been sharp. She rarely showed it, preferring to earn adoration for her fashion sense and general beauty, but I'd always seen that a lot went on in her mind. When our cousin Rose had first come to stay with us, Catherine had been suspicious. She'd suspected things of Rose that I hadn't seen—though I'd still been rather young at the time.

Catherine paid close attention to those around her and saw things others didn't, but to my knowledge, those "things" had never been spirits walking amongst us.

"Are you sure?" I asked. "She has told you she sees ghosts?"

"Yes." Charles' voice broke, and he dropped his face into his hands. "I want to believe her. She is my wife, and I've always trusted her option, but this? This is beyond rational thought. It is beyond...our world. Catherine begs me to see things her way, but how can I, Alice?"

I laid a hand on his shoulder. "I'm sorry, Charles. I wish I'd known sooner."

"I thought it would go away on its own," he admitted. "Knowing nothing of pregnancy, I thought hysterics might be one of the symptoms. Something to do with exhaustion. So, I did my best to make Catherine comfortable in hopes things would ease when the baby arrived. I thought the joy of our child would distract Catherine from her feelings and put everything right again, but..."

Charles looked up at the house, and I could see the loss in his eyes. It was a grief...a mourning for what could have been.

"But things grew worse?"

"Much worse. Much, much worse." He dropped his hands and rested his head back against the seat, his eyes closed. "The birth was traumatic. The doctor barely delivered the baby alive, and Catherine lost so much blood. I thought I was going to lose them both."

Charles had always been a stoic man, so seeing his lip tremble with emotion brought a sudden mistiness to my own eyes. I blinked it away, trying to remain strong. For him and for Catherine.

"But she is all right?"

"Physically, yes," he reiterated. "The doctor successfully delivered Hazel and tended to Catherine. She was so strong, Alice. You would have been proud. Catherine nursed our baby within an hour after delivery, even while she could barley open her eyes. I'd never seen such strength. Such resilience. The doctor, too, was amazed by her tenacity."

"That sounds like Catherine," I said with a small smile. Charles returned it, but the memory leeched away, light and color draining from his eyes like the setting sun.

"Having Hazel has helped pull Catherine through, I'm sure, but she hasn't fixed everything."

"Is Catherine still seeing things?" I looked back to the house just as a shadow moved across an upstairs window. Whoever had been standing there was gone now, but the curtain swayed in their wake. I wondered if it was Catherine.

Charles shrugged. "I think so, but she won't tell me anything. Not anymore. I've lost her trust."

"How?"

"By not moving our family as soon as she asked."

"She was pregnant," I said, reaching out to comfort

him once again. "Moving would have been a large upheaval. Surely Catherine doesn't blame you for staying."

"She didn't until the accident."

I pulled my hand back and blinked. "What accident?"

Rather than answer my question, Charles threw open his door and climbed out of the car. He reached into the backseat to free my case from where it was wedged. We met at the front of the car, the engine making clicking sounds at it cooled down from the drive.

"What accident?" I repeated.

"I'll let Catherine tell you more," he said. "No one knows what happened out there. Maybe not even Catherine. But she will not talk to me about it anymore."

I looked back up at the house, wishing I could know all of its secrets. Instead of answers, I saw only cracks in the façade. From a distance, they were not visible, but up close, things were beginning to flake away. Paint chipped around the window frames, weeds grew up in boxes where flowers had once been, and dust collected on the steps and the walkway with no one to sweep it away.

The house was of a good size and build, but the vastness of the heather fields seemed to overwhelm it. Rather than sitting proudly on the hill, the ground seemed to be wrapped around the edges of the house, swallowing it up bit by bit until there would be nothing left soon.

I couldn't be certain how much of my assessment was based upon the ominous information Charles had just divulged, but the fact remained either way: the house gave me an eerie feeling, and I couldn't blame Catherine for wanting to get away.

When Charles pushed open the front door and

ushered me inside, I had to admit the interior of the home felt much cozier than the exterior.

There was a large stone fireplace in the sitting room to the right of the entrance, and I could imagine a nice evening curled up in one of the armchairs, a book in hand. Charles' study sat behind glass French doors across the hall, and a dining room with a large wooden table and chairs was a bit further down. It was a comfortable home with a lot of potential for entertaining, which made it all the more strange that it was almost perfectly silent.

Then, there was the sound of water splashing, and I turned towards a swinging door that had to have been the kitchen. There were indeed other people in the house, though it didn't sound like a full staff. Rather, it sounded like a single person doing the washing up.

"We want you to make yourself at home and stay as long as you like," Charles said. He sounded more cheerful than he had outside, and when I looked up, he had a polite smile stretched across his face. I could see that it was false right away, but it was obvious he was trying.

I followed his lead and smiled in return. "Thank you. Is my room to be upstairs?"

"Yes, the maid readied your room this morning, so I will take your bags upstairs and allow you to get settled."

He must have seen my frown and understood its reason. "Our staff here is small, but they are all efficient and loyal. Anything you require will be found and provided within reason."

"Oh, what a shame. I planned to be entirely unreasonable."

Charles looked over his shoulder at me and blinked

for a second before he smiled. Clearly, he hadn't been in a joking mood for a very long time. Then, he carried my luggage upstairs and bid me follow him. We were halfway up the stairs when I heard the humming.

The sound was faint, but the melody dipped low and held, singing mournful, slow notes. The song settled in my chest like a stone, threatening to drag me down. Suddenly, I didn't want to go upstairs at all.

If Catherine was humming that kind of song, I didn't want to go any further.

"My sister," Charles said quietly. "She is in with the baby. I'll introduce you later. She doesn't like to be disturbed."

My relief was replaced by questions—why was Charles' sister already here if I'd only just been called for? And why would she hum a song like that to the baby?

Before I could ask any questions at all, Charles set down my case in front of a door and nodded towards it. "Your room during your stay."

I thanked him, but then Charles added, "Catherine's room is at the end of the hall if you wish to see her first."

I'd wanted nothing more than to see my sister for weeks. I'd been desperate to get to her and learn the source of her troubles, but now my stomach dropped at the prospect. It all felt so real and personal. More than that, the idea of seeing Catherine in any kind of distress was unfamiliar to me. She'd always been strong and capable and tough.

I didn't want to view my older sister in another way.

I debated my answer for only a second before I bent down, grabbed my case, and turned the handle of my door. "I want to freshen up before seeing her. I'm dusty from travel."

Charles didn't say anything, but he looked disappointed as he bowed his head and turned for the stairs. I shut my door quickly and pressed my back against it, taking deep breaths.

I didn't believe in ghosts in the slightest, but being in this house gave me doubts. Five minutes inside, and I'd been reduced to a shivering coward.

What could be the explanation for that?

3

The guest room had a small fireplace and embers glowed in the center, signifying a once burning fire. The first thing I did was lay a couple small logs into the hearth and poke them around until the embers could be coaxed back into life. Warm flames licked at the dry wood as I walked a small circle around the room, admiring the space.

Or rather, inspecting it.

The plaster around the window was cracked, and I could feel a distinct breeze coming through the window and rattling the glass panes. Thankfully, after several weeks of sleeping on a ship with very thin walls, I didn't think I'd have much trouble falling asleep.

Thick quilts were laid over the bed and the pillows were fluffed, but dust had collected in the corners of the room and the headboard and bedside table were both scratched and dented from years of use. The items looked too old to have been bought new by Charles and

Catherine after their wedding. Had they been purchased with the house?

Regardless, they were in need of repair, and I wondered who was in charge of such things. Certainly not Charles. Though, I couldn't truly discount it as an option.

I changed out of my walking skirt and jacket, and put on a pink cotton dress and long tan sweater, instead. Even if my surroundings were dreary and gray, I wanted to look cheerful. That was why I'd been called here, after all. To cheer Catherine up to the best of my abilities. A pop of color seemed like a good place to start.

Just after I'd buckled my shoes, Charles knocked at the door. I took a steadying breath, pressed a smile on, and met him in the hallway.

"I don't mean to rush you. If you'd like to rest before we go in, then I'm sure Catherine would under—"

"No, I'm ready," I said cheerfully. "I was just coming to look for you."

That wasn't true at all. If left undisturbed, I could have stayed in the room for an hour or more. Out of all the things I'd faced, having to be an emotional encouragement to my sister frightened me the most.

Charles walked towards Catherine's door, but hesitated just outside, his hand hovering over the knob. Then, as if mustering his confidence, he nodded once and then pushed the door open.

I followed him in and then stopped in the doorway, mouth open.

The room was dark—the curtains pulled closed and the lights all low—but I could make out the shape of a woman in

bed. Blankets were pulled up to her neck, her arms mummi-
fied to her sides. The only reason I could tell it was Catherine
was because of the blonde curls that spilled across the blanket, longer than I'd seen them since I was a little girl.

"Mrs. Cresswell is resting."

Another figure I hadn't seen rose from a chair in the
corner and stalked towards us, and I jumped back in
surprise. Charles, too, I noticed, jumped.

"I'm sure she'll want to wake long enough to see her
sister," Charles said.

The woman—petite with long gray hair twisted into a
bun and a somber black dress—shook her head and
grabbed the door, pushing it half-closed on us. Charles
took a step back to avoid being hit and knocked me into
the hallway.

"I'll find you when she wakes."

Charles opened his mouth to argue, but the woman
closed the door on us both, and I heard it lock from the
other side.

I would have been more surprised by the strange
woman forcing Charles from a room in his own home—a
room his wife was sleeping in—if I hadn't been so
shocked by the sight of Catherine in the bed.

It was hard to tell beneath the covers whether she
looked well or if she was thin, but even in sleep, I saw the
dark circles beneath her eyes. I saw the pale color of her
lips and the thin quality to her skin.

She looked ill.

"You said she was physically healthy," I said, staring at
the door like I could see through it.

Charles let out a breath and turned for the stairs. I

followed him several seconds later, not knowing what else to do.

"She is," he said. "It is her mind that causes her trouble. Sleeping helps her."

Of course, sleeping helped. Because she was unconscious while sleeping. No one could talk about hallucinations and seeing ghosts if they weren't awake to see them.

"How often does she sleep each day?" I asked.

Charles walked into his study, leaving the door open behind him. He dropped down into his chair with a sigh and ran a hand down his face. There appeared to be a patch of gray hairs clustered at his temple, hiding amongst the blonde. "She takes several naps."

"Every day?" I asked, trying to remember a time when Catherine had ever napped. "That cannot be normal. Have you spoken with a doctor? Sleeping that much could signify another issue? She looked pale. Perhaps, she is suffering with some illness and it is making her tired and delirious and—"

"She is given a sleeping draught several times a day," Charles explained, holding up a hand to quiet my rush of concerns. "She takes it willingly, and it makes things easier."

"On whom?" The charge was out of my mouth before I could pull it back in, and for the first time since we met at the train station, Charles didn't look sad or tired. He looked angry.

His nostrils flared, and he stood up, palms flat on the desk. "I've done everything I can to care for your sister— my wife—and I am doing my best. There is a new baby to look after—"

"Who I still haven't seen yet," I added. I'd only just

arrived, and biting my tongue seemed like the wise thing to do in this case, but I couldn't do it. Not after seeing my sister wasting away in a dark bedroom. "And who was the woman in the room with her?"

"Nurse Gray," Charles snapped back. "She has been caring for Catherine diligently for months."

"Have you seen improvement?"

Charles pressed his lips together, and I knew the answer.

"Has she grown worse?"

His lips were mashed together so tightly they were white. I pinched the bridge of my nose and shook my head. "Something must be done, Charles. Catherine is wasting away up there."

"You've only just arrived, Alice!" Charles snapped.

I stepped back, surprised by the outburst, and Charles released a sharp exhale through his nose. Then, he flopped down into his chair. "I'm sorry, but you don't know the entire situation, Alice. Ask Catherine. Go and speak with her for yourself, and you'll see what I mean. I didn't know what else to do."

"I would speak with her, but there is a woman guarding her bed." My voice was still sharp, but I looked down at the floor as I delivered the words. I wanted to be angry and blame someone for the uncomfortable scene I'd witnessed, but it was clear to me that person couldn't be Charles. He looked like a man fresh from battle, battered and exhausted. He needed help, which was why I'd been asked to come. Not to beat up on him even more. "I'm sorry."

He waved my apology away. "Just try and help your sister. Please."

"I'll try my best."

And I would.

As SHE SAID SHE WOULD, Nurse Gray came down half an hour later to tell Charles that Catherine was awake. I overheard the announcement and rose from where I'd been waiting on the sofa in the sitting room.

When Nurse Gray turned from Charles' study door to go back upstairs, she studied me with narrowed, assessing eyes for a second and then disappeared without a formal introduction.

"You go on ahead," Charles said. "Catherine will be anxious to see you."

"Don't you want to come with me?" I didn't know why, but I was nervous to go and see my sister on my own. Charles had said repeatedly she wasn't ill, but Catherine looked ill lying in that bed, and I'd never been good around the ailing or grieving. The humanity of it left me feeling small and inconsequential, and I never knew what to say.

Charles shook his head. "I'll see Catherine later. You are the one she has been waiting for. Go ahead. Nurse Gray won't throw you out of the room for awhile yet. You'd better see Catherine while you can."

His mouth turned up in a small smile, letting me know he was only teasing, but I wondered how much of it was a joke? Considering Nurse Gray had just thrown us both out of the room half an hour ago, I took Charles at his word and walked up the stairs to see my sister.

The door was cracked open, and I could hear voices

on the other side. I hesitated outside the door to try and listen in on the conversation, perhaps hear something that would help me better understand what was happening in this house.

As soon as I pressed my ear to the door, however, the voices stopped.

"You may come in," Nurse Gray said.

My cheeks reddened, and I pushed the door open and stepped inside.

"Still eavesdropping after all these years?" Catherine's voice was creaky from sleep, and her eyelids were still heavy, but she was sitting up in bed now, the blankets pooled around her waist. "Will you ever grow out of those nasty habits?"

"Never," I said, grinning as I crossed the room.

I could see now that Catherine was not thin or undernourished. In fact, she was still slightly round in the middle from having given birth only a few weeks prior. Still, her lips were dry and colorless. As if reading my mind, she licked them and waved for me to sit next to her on the bed.

As I approached, I looked to Nurse Gray, expecting her to tell me to keep my distance, but even though it looked like that was exactly what she wanted to say, my sister's nurse sat back in her rocking chair and took up her knitting.

"I'm so glad you're here, Alice. I've missed you." Catherine grabbed my hand, and I couldn't remember the last time we'd shared such an intimate moment.

My relationship with my sister had always been warm, but we teased one another and played. Rarely ever did we divulge our deepest feelings. It felt strange, but given the circumstances, I indulged.

"I've missed you, too," I said. "I came the second I received your telegram. I would have come sooner if you'd only told me..."

Told me what? That she was having hallucinations? That she was seeing ghosts?

The possibilities hung in the air between us, and I couldn't give voice to any of them. I wanted Catherine to tell me the truth from her perspective.

"I can see by the look on your face that Charles has already spoken with you." Catherine still wore a smile, but it was wistful, and she couldn't hold my gaze. "I'm all right, Alice. Really."

Nurse Gray took that moment to clear her throat, and I didn't know whether it was a coincidence or her way of letting me know Catherine was not all right. Either way, I ignored it.

I wanted to tell the woman to leave, but it was Catherine's room and she was Catherine's nurse, and it didn't feel like my place.

"There is no look on my face. I'm just tired from travelling," I lied. "I've been on a ship for too many days to count. I'm not even sure what month it is."

Catherine rolled her eyes, but even that small movement seemed to cost her energy. "Did you write to Mama and Papa before coming?"

"Actually, I stayed with them for a night."

Catherine's eyes went wide, and for the first time since coming into the room, I caught a glimpse of the same level of alarm that had been in her telegram. The look was gone in an instant, but I'd seen it. She was afraid to know what I'd told them.

"I told them I wanted to come and visit you and Hazel. Mama wanted me to wait and come with her and Papa later, but I simply explained we needed some time alone as sisters, and they understood."

"Papa maybe, but certainly not Mama." Catherine laughed. "I'm surprised you made it out of the house at all."

"Me too," I admitted.

I wanted to ask Catherine what she'd been doing lately and how little Hazel was, but based on what I'd seen and heard thus far, my sister hadn't been doing much beyond sleeping in this room. I was afraid if Catherine had to voice that reality, she would be embarrassed. So, instead of asking her questions, I talked about myself.

I told Catherine about my time in New York, leaving out the more excitable bits since Nurse Gray was still hovering in the corner, and about the letter I'd received from Sherborne Sharp.

"Did you write him back?"

I nodded. "Just before coming here. I'm sure he has gotten it by now."

"Did you tell him you loved him, too?" Catherine's eyes were wide and bright. She looked almost like the sister I'd always known. Almost.

I furrowed my brow. "Why would I say a silly thing like that? He didn't tell me he loved me. It wouldn't make any sense."

"He nearly said it," she scoffed. "He told you he cares

about your safety and misses you when you aren't around. That is love, dear little sister."

"It's friendship!"

Again, Catherine rolled her eyes and pursed her lips. "I've failed you as an older sister. Really, you should know better than that."

She teased me a bit more before I managed to turn the subject back to my time in New York City, which unfortunately included the death of one of Catherine's old friends.

"I'm sorry to have told you the information in a telegram, but I didn't know what else to do," I said. "I didn't want you to find out some other way before a letter could arrive."

Catherine laid her hand over mine and squeezed. "I'm just glad you told me. And I'm sorry you found her. That must have been horrible."

Moisture filled my eyes, and I blinked it away. It had been weeks since the accident, and I hadn't known the woman as well as Catherine had. Still, the trauma felt fresh in my mind, and I hadn't realized until that moment how badly I'd needed someone to hold my hand and tell me all would be well.

"Mrs. Cresswell?"

We both jumped at Nurse Gray's voice, having forgotten she was there.

Somehow, she'd silently stood from her chair and walked towards us without making a sound.

"Perhaps it is time to rest," the nurse suggested.

Catherine's shoulders fell in disappointment, and I looked from my sister to her nurse and back again, trying to understand their dynamic. I waited for Catherine to say something, to tell her nurse to leave us alone for a few moments. But she didn't say anything.

My outspoken sister, who had always let people know exactly what she thought about them regardless of how it would embarrass or shame them, nodded her head in solemn agreement.

The scene was so absurd I could have laughed.

"I thought we could go for a walk before the sun sets," I said suddenly, squeezing Catherine's fingers before she could pull her hand away. "It is a lovely day."

"A bit brisk," Nurse Gray cut in.

"Nothing a warm shawl can't fix." I smiled at the nurse, and I hoped she could see the malice behind it. Whatever was going on in this house, I had the distinct feeling my sister's nurse was doing more harm than good.

At my push back, Catherine seemed to come alive a bit. She sat up straighter and pushed her blankets aside. "Actually, I think a walk would be very good for me. I can't remember the last time I was outside."

"This morning," Nurse Gray said. "I wheeled you out to the patio."

Wheeled?

Catherine looked at me out of the corner of her eye, and then shook her head as if to dismiss a thought. "I would like to walk. I'm strong enough."

I helped my sister shrug into a coat and shoes, and then she promptly stood up, grabbed my arm, and pulled me towards the door. "Come on, Alice. Let's go."

She was so determined, and I enjoyed the look of shock on Nurse Gray's face so much that I didn't mention to my sister that she was about to go on a walk through the moors of Yorkshire in her nightgown.

4

"We should go back." Catherine wrapped her arms around herself, pulling her coat closed so only the bottom of her white nightgown hung out of the coat. "I look ridiculous."

"No one can see you." I spun in a circle, gesturing to the empty moors around us. "It's just the two of us. Besides, it is nice to finally be alone."

Catherine sighed and walked ahead of me a bit.

In the house, she'd seemed weak and pale and ill. She still looked pale, but she no longer looked weak. She looked capable to me. Which begged the question, why was she being put to sleep several times a day?

"Who is Nurse Gray?" I asked.

Catherine shrugged and stepped up onto a rock that had broken through the mossy ground, balancing on one foot before stepping back to the damp earth. "She came right after Hazel was born, and she never left."

"The delivery didn't go well?"

"They told me I lost a lot of blood. That I was lucky to be alive. I don't remember any of it. I just remember waking up and seeing Nurse Gray."

I frowned. "Do you always call her that? What is her full name?"

"She asks me to call her Nurse Gray. Keeping the separation of personal and professional is very important to her. So, I am Mrs. Cresswell, and she is Nurse Gray."

"But she has been here for weeks?" I asked.

Catherine looked up at the heavy, gray sky, brow wrinkled in thought. "It doesn't feel like that long, but yes. It has been a few weeks, I think."

If Nurse Gray had been there since Hazel was born then Catherine should have known exactly how long the woman had been in the house. What mother didn't know the age of her own child?

A mother who had been drugged three times a day and kept unconscious.

"How is Hazel? Charles said he nearly lost you both during the birth. Is everything all right with her?"

Catherine nodded. "The cord was around her neck, but as soon as they got it free, Hazel was fine. She is progressing well."

Progressing?

Prior to the birth, Catherine had talked excitedly about being a mother. About what it would be like to hold her child. She wondered whether the child would look more like Charles or herself, whether it would be a boy or a girl. There had been a shine in her voice that was noticeably absent now.

Her words were cold and factual. Distant.

The muddy trail from the back of the house broke into three as it neared a crop of trees, and I walked towards the one on the left.

"Not that way," Catherine said, grabbing my arm.

She pointed to a large rock positioned on the far-right trail. It had a wide base and the tip had been sharpened into a point. "Charles put that rock there so I wouldn't forget which path was safest. He walked all of these trails right after..." Her voice trailed off before she picked up the sentence again. "...and that one has the widest path and avoids the crumbling rock falls."

"After what?"

Catherine raised her brows at me as if she didn't hear my question, but I knew she had. She was trying to avoid answering it, and I wanted to know why.

"Charles walked these trails after what?" I repeated. "What happened, Catherine? Why did you ask me to come here?"

My sister stared at me, her eyebrows drawn together in concern. Then, she shook her head and turned away, a strand of frizzy blonde hair curling around her cheek.

She wasn't herself. Nothing about the woman in front of me seemed familiar anymore. It seemed as though, since the last time I'd seen her, someone had reached inside of her chest and snuffed out the light in her heart. The light that used to annoy me to no end, but that I suddenly wished I could find again.

"What is happening, Catherine?" I fisted my hands at my side, trying to keep my fingers from trembling. "You've asked me to come here and nothing makes sense. Charles was a mess in the car. Your husband talks about you like you're dying, you barely see your daughter or seem to care that you don't see her, and an old woman is ordering you around and putting you to sleep. What does any of this mean? Is it because of your hallucinations? Are you mad?"

Catherine's head snapped up at that, her blue eyes sparkling with tears. "Do you think I'm mad?"

"This is all so bizarre, I'm starting to think *I'm* mad!" My voice echoed off the trees, coming back to me in a faded whisper, and I let out a long breath.

Suddenly, Catherine was in front of me, her head low. "I asked you here to help me, but now that you're here, I'm afraid you'll look at me the way everyone else does. And if that happens, Alice, I'm not sure what I'll do. You are my last hope."

My throat tightened at the desperation in her voice, and I grabbed my sister by the shoulders and pulled her towards me. She sagged against me, limp for a second before she succumbed to the embrace and wrapped her arms around me.

"I'm here to help, Catherine. Tell me how."

Catherine pulled back and nodded. "It started when I was pregnant. I thought it was nerves because of the baby, but the more it happened, the more I couldn't deny it."

"Deny what?" I felt I already knew the answer, but I wanted to hear Catherine's explanation.

"Ghosts." She blinked. "I could see ghosts, Alice. Well, I can."

Cold air prickled the back of my neck, lifting the hairs there. "Still?"

Catherine nodded again, her eyes darting from mine to the sky and to the ground. She was nervous.

"Right now?" I looked back over my shoulder.

"No," she said through a small laugh. "Not right now. I wouldn't be standing here if I saw a ghost right now."

"So, that means you're afraid of them?"

"Wouldn't you be?" Catherine raised her brows, waiting for an answer.

I would be. The problem was, I'd never believed in ghosts. I enjoyed hearing a ghost story shared in front of a fire, but I'd never seen anything to make me believe spirits wandered the Earth. So, there had to be an explanation for what Catherine had been seeing.

"What do the ghosts look like?"

"I can't always see them. Sometimes there is just a feeling in the air. A chill and a creepy feeling in my stomach."

I turned to look at the house through the tree branches. The windows on the side of the house rattled in the wind off the moors. I remembered the gust I'd felt in my room upon arrival. "The house is drafty, Cat. It's an old place. It could just be—"

"I know what wind feels like." Catherine turned away from me and walked to the edge of the path. "And I know you think I'm insane. Everyone does. Even when I nearly died, no one believed me."

I snapped my attention back to her. "What do you mean you nearly died? Are you talking about the birth? Do you think a ghost complicated Hazel's birth, because Catherine, that *is* madness."

"No," she snapped, spinning back around. Her coat had fallen open, revealing the white cotton of her nightgown, and Catherine looked a bit like a ghost herself. The dying light of the sun cast the grounds in a blue light, and her nightgown seemed to glow. That, paired with the paleness of her skin, made her seem spectral. "Hazel's birth was complicated for natural reasons, I know that. But during my recovery, I was weak and exhausted, but I was still conscious. I could hear things. I heard Charles weeping next to my bed in worry. I heard him tell Nurse Gray to do all she could to save me. I heard Charles' sister say it wasn't safe to allow me around the baby."

"I'm sure she didn't mean that."

Catherine shook her head. "No one trusted me. They didn't trust me around the baby, and they didn't trust me when I told them what I saw."

"What did you see?" I whispered.

Catherine looked back at the house, and I realized I could see her window from our position. She had a perfect view of the trails from her room.

"Flashes of movement in the trees," she said. "Charles told me they were dreams, but I know what I saw. I saw smoke and hooded figures. They looked up at my window in the night and chanted things to me. When I tried to open my window, they disappeared."

Catherine sounded certain. Confident of what she'd seen.

But it was impossible...wasn't it?

I could allow for shadows moving in the trees. That could have been any number of wild animals scouring the moors for their supper. But hooded figures and chants were more difficult to explain away. Those were not a trick of the eye, but a trick of the mind.

"I saw them again. In person," Catherine said, moving closer to me. Her eyes locked on mine. "Nurse Gray said what I saw was an effect of the medication, but once I had regained my strength and was going for daily walks, I didn't need the medication anymore. My mind was clear, and I saw a hooded figure in the flesh."

I knew Catherine could see the doubt in my eyes because I could see the hurt in hers. She wanted me to believe her so badly, and I wanted to believe her, too. She was my sister, and I wanted to be on her side, but I also couldn't indulge these visions until I knew what they were. I couldn't blindly tell her I believed her when I had no proof to back it up.

Catherine was standing so close to me I could feel her breath on my face, but I didn't pull away. Even if I didn't believe her story, I wanted her to know I wasn't going to run away. I wouldn't flee back to London and leave her here with her nurse and her overwhelmed husband. I wouldn't leave until things were right in Catherine's world, whatever that meant.

"Charles thinks I grew weak from my walk and struck my head," Catherine said, turning her head and lifting her hair to reveal a still-red wound behind her ear. The cut was jagged and fresh, though mostly closed now. "He thinks I fell, landed on a rock, and had a dream. But I know the truth."

"What is the truth?"

"I was attacked," Catherine whispered. Her blue eyes went glassy with emotion, and she reached out and took my hands. "I felt the blow to my head and saw the flash of the robes. Whatever spirits remain here, they do not want us on this land. They want us to leave. If we don't, they'll try again. I know they will."

My sister glanced over her shoulder towards the trail that had gone dark as the sun sank below the horizon. I saw a shiver work down her spine, and I reached out to comfort her.

Immediately, Catherine jerked away from my touch. "I'm not mad, Alice. I know you and Edward always thought I was silly because I liked pretty things and going to parties. None of that makes me simple-minded."

"I know that, Catherine. I've never thought—"

She held up a hand to quiet me. "I've only ever wanted a peaceful, comfortable life, so I would not make a story like this up. My first thought when it all started was that I was seeing things. But I can't believe that is true anymore. I've seen and experienced too much, and now I know the truth: we have to leave this place, or we'll all die."

I wanted to say too much. I wanted to tell Catherine that I'd always admired her and that neither Edward nor I ever thought she was simple. I wanted to tell her I loved her and I was worried for her. I wanted to tell her she should go inside and rest, but I didn't want to sound like Nurse Gray or Charles.

More than anything, I wanted to tell Catherine that everything would be fine, but I didn't know that for sure. Not because I thought she was in danger of being attacked by a spirit, but because if she truly believed that was possible, perhaps her mind had gone.

The thought wasn't so preposterous.

I never would have guessed our brother would be a convicted murderer, yet he'd confessed to the crimes. Compared to that, Catherine losing her sense of reality didn't seem impossible. In fact, it seemed likely. After everything our family had been through over the years, it made sense that someone would break under the pressure.

I just thought it would be our mother before it would be Catherine.

"Mrs. Cresswell?"

Nurse Gray's approaching voice brought me a sense of comfort. I needed time to process what Catherine had revealed and decide how to move forward. But when I saw the disappointed look in my sister's eyes, I felt like a traitor.

"Over here, Nurse Gray." Catherine gave me one last look before her shoulders slouched forward.

Nurse Gray mounted the slight incline to where we stood with ease for someone so advanced in years. She gave her full attention to Catherine, barely noticing me at all. "Dinner is ready, Mrs. Cresswell. Mr. Cresswell had a plate delivered to your room."

"Charles?" Betrayal flashed in her eyes.

Nurse Gray nodded. "He thought you'd be tired from your walk."

I wanted to argue, but I'd overstepped enough boundaries in my short time in my sister's home. Anyway, I was no longer sure the measures Nurse Gray and Charles had taken were unwarranted.

If Catherine was delusional, she needed more rest.

"I am tired," Catherine sighed. "Thank you."

She walked up to the house next to Nurse Gray, and I trailed behind them. When we got into the house, Nurse Gray led Catherine upstairs without another word, and I watched them go.

Even though I wanted to say a great many things, for

one of the first times in my life, I simply couldn't find the words.

5

A s it turned out, dinner wasn't ready.

Not for the rest of the house, anyway.

Despite her having taken several naps throughout the day already, Charles thought Catherine would like to go to bed early, so he had her dinner prepared ahead of time. Which meant I had an hour of spare time to use up before dinner.

Sitting with Catherine while she ate was an option, but I didn't want to embarrass her if she didn't realize her dinner had been prepared special ahead of everyone else's. Besides, I still didn't know what to say to her.

Catherine wanted me to believe her so badly, but I simply couldn't. Hooded figures and chants and vengeful spirits...it all seemed like fiction. Like a frightening story told to children, not something that could really happen.

Charles remained in his study on the first floor with the door closed, showing no sign of interest in mingling with his guest, and the rest of the small household staff seemed otherwise engaged.

So, I explored the house.

In addition to the sitting room, study, dining room, and kitchen, the main floor boasted a library, as well. A quick assessment of the shelves told me that most of the books belonged to Charles. Volume after volume of world maps were not the kind of light reading Catherine usually engaged in. Still, I found a not insignificant section of novels that would be entertaining to me should I find the time to read them.

One copy, creased and folded back from use, caught my eye, and I pulled the book from the shelf. *Wuthering Heights*.

Catherine had never been one for reading, and I couldn't imagine Charles reading the doomed love affair of Heathcliff and the fictional Catherine. I peeled back the cover and noticed the delicately scrawled inscription.

To my dearest Catherine

May our home on the moors be the opposite of Wuthering Heights in every way. May it be warm and safe and welcome. May it be filled to the brim with love as I am filled to the brim with love for you.

Yours always,
*   Charles*

I couldn't say exactly why, but tears sprang to my eyes at the warmth in the writing. At the hopes Charles had for their life in this new house and the juxtaposition of what had passed.

I blinked the emotion away and flipped through the pages.

Immediately, I was caught by the writing in the margins. At the lines scrawled under passages, underlining things deemed to be important.

On that bleak hill-top the earth was hard with a black frost, and the air made me shiver through every limb.

The dismal spiritual atmosphere overcame, and more than neutralized, the glowing physical comforts around me...

The encounter Lockwood had with Catherine's ghost at the window was so scribbled over that I could barely read the passage anymore. Clearly, whoever read the book last had felt something in kind with the narrator's experience. I didn't allow myself to think what my sister must have looked like, stooped over this book, underlining line after line after line.

To think she could have so much in common with such a book brought a fresh wave of emotion, and I closed the book and slid it back on the shelf.

I had to help her. Whatever was going on, I had to do my best to ease her mind and bring back some of the happiness they'd experienced when they'd purchased the place. Clearly, Charles had great hopes for their time spent here and the family they would build, and if neither of them could figure out how to navigate their way out of this tangled wood, I would have to lead the way.

There seemed only one right place to start.

A SOFT HUMMING STILL SOUNDED from beneath the door

of Hazel's nursery, but I hadn't seen any person come or go from the room since I'd arrived.

Strange, considering Charles and Catherine's newborn child was in there. My niece.

Charles had said his sister was watching over the baby, but he'd also mentioned a nanny was on staff. I wasn't sure who I would find on the other side of the door, but I knocked anyway, and waited.

The humming stopped, cutting off abruptly, and I heard footsteps. When the door cracked open, I could just see a single eye through the crack. It narrowed at the sight of me.

"Hello, I'm Alice," I said, smiling despite the strangeness of the encounter. "Catherine's sister. I thought I would come and meet the baby."

The eye was pale blue, almost white, and it unsettled me. That feeling only grew as the silence stretched on.

"I'm sorry, are you the nanny?" I asked. "Should I go and fetch Charles? I'm sure he wouldn't mind me meeting my niece, but if I need permission, I'm willing to go and get it."

Suddenly, the door opened, and a petite woman stood in front of me, a swaddled baby in her arms.

"No permission needed," she said softly. "I simply forgot you were coming to visit us today, and it took me a moment to find my manners. The baby is sleeping, so perhaps you could come back—"

"I'll be quiet." I stepped into the nursery, careful to keep my heels from sounding on the wood floors. I turned in the middle of the room and repeated my earlier question. "Are you the nanny?"

The woman had light brown hair that hung to her

shoulders in limp curls. It didn't look like it had been styled or combed in days. Everything in the house, it seemed, had fallen into some form of disrepair.

"No, no," she shook her head. "I'm Camellia Cresswell, Charles' older sister."

I thought I remembered Charles' sister being a married woman, though I couldn't remember what Catherine had said her married name was. It was surprising that she still called herself Cresswell, but I supposed it was none of my business.

"Oh, so we are both aunts to this wonderful little bundle." I nodded towards the baby in her arms, stretching onto my toes to try and get a peek of my niece's precious face.

Camellia's smile faltered before returning, bigger and broader than before. "Yes, I suppose so. Charles asked me to come shortly after the birth. Things didn't go well, as I'm sure you know. Catherine tried, poor thing, but some women are not built for childbirth I'm afraid. It is a wonder she survived the experience at all."

Camellia smiled down at Hazel as she spoke, admiring the child, and I couldn't help but think she didn't sound at all upset about the tragic birth.

I pushed the thought away as soon as I'd considered it. I barely knew this woman, and aside from thinking she loved my sister's baby slightly too much, I had no reason to suspect her of anything. Besides, Camellia couldn't have arranged for the cord to be wrapped around Hazel's neck even if she did wish my sister ill.

"Thank God she recovered," I said. "I wish someone had told me of the troubles she was going through. I would have come sooner."

Camellia turned away and strolled back towards the rocking chair, swaying Hazel gently in her arms, and then lowered down into the seat. "Charles likes to keep his personal life private. He thought he could manage the entire situation himself, but brought me in when it became clear he couldn't."

I wanted to point out that I was family. That involving me would not have been the same as going public with the information. But I had a feeling Camellia understood that and had made her statement in hopes of delineating our roles within the house.

She wanted me to know that she was trusted, and that I was nothing more than a guest.

"Thank goodness you were available to help. How long have you been here?"

Camellia blinked, and her eyes seemed to go blank. Her mouth fell into a flat line, and her attention fixated just over my shoulder. "Two and a half months."

Almost since the beginning. Had Camellia been caring for the child by herself that entire time? Catherine said she heard Camellia tell her brother it wasn't safe for Catherine to be around the baby. How long had she been keeping Catherine separate from her child, and how could Charles let this happen?

"That is a long time. Doesn't your own family miss you?" I asked, hoping to discover exactly what Camellia's family looked like. Did the woman have a husband and children of her own?

Again, Camellia blinked, and her gaze shifted to me. She shook her head numbly. "No. I'm afraid I miss them far more than they miss me."

Her words were a puzzle I didn't have time to solve.

The only reason I'd come up to the room at all was to ensure Hazel Cresswell was alive and well. Until I'd seen her in Camellia's arms, I couldn't dismiss the possibility that the child had actually been lost during the delivery and the entire house was under some kind of delusion.

Talk about a plot better suited for a Victorian novel. That would have been a rather bleak story, indeed.

Thankfully, the child seemed to be fine, if overly protected by her paternal aunt, and there was hope yet of reuniting my sister's family.

"Is there any chance I could hold the child?" I asked. "This is the first time I've seen her, and—"

Before I could get the question out, the door opened, and a young woman with pitch dark hair pinned over her ears and a simple gray dress came in. "I'm here for Hazel, if it is all right? Dinner is ready downstairs, and Mr. Cresswell has asked that you both join him."

"Of course." Camellia stood at once and handed the baby off to the woman, who I assumed was the nanny.

Before I could ask the servant's name, Camellia pressed a hand to the center of my back and guided me gently, yet firmly from the room.

"YOU TWO HAVE ALREADY BEEN ACQUAINTED, I see." Charles sat at the head of the table and stood as his sister and I entered. "It feels good to have both of my sisters under the same roof."

"Alice came into the nursery." Camellia was smiling, but it felt like she was telling on me, hoping Charles would chastise me for wandering the house unsupervised.

"My niece sleeps almost as much as my sister," I said, taking my seat to the left of Charles while Camellia sat on his right. I had thought the seat would be reserved for Catherine, even though she wasn't joining us. "I was hoping to catch her awake and finally make her acquaintance."

Charles pressed his lips together. "I'm sure it will happen soon enough. Though, I hardly see her between Camellia and the nanny. They both dote on her."

"But nothing can replace the love of a father," I said warmly, hoping he understood the not so subtle meaning.

Hazel should be cared for by her parents. By her mother and her father.

I'd been brought to the house to speak with Catherine, but I wouldn't mind speaking with Charles, as well. It seemed he needed someone to point out to him that he was no longer running his home.

"Certainly," Camellia agreed. "Hazel is fortunate to have a father who looks out for her interests and does what is best for her regardless."

Charles smiled at his sister, and I suddenly didn't feel so hungry.

I didn't know what I'd expected to find upon arriving in Yorkshire, but it wasn't this.

A nurse who dosed my potentially insane sister to sleep while her daughter was cared for by her sister-in-law and her husband encouraged the whole mess? I never ever could have predicted that.

"How many visitors do you all receive out here?" I asked.

Charles seemed taken aback by the question and frowned. "I'm not sure. I go into town for meetings occasionally and am always sure to call on a few acquaintances when I—"

"Here," I repeated. "How many people come and visit at the house?"

He sliced off a piece of roast, took a bite, and shook his head. "No one aside from you and Camellia for a good while."

"And the neighbors once," Camellia added. "Just after I arrived the Wilds came to welcome me to the area."

"The Wilds?"

Camellia laughed, grabbing her brother's arm at some private joke. "That is their name."

"Margaret and Abigail Wilds," Charles clarified. "They live two miles up the road. Though, we usually pay them visits. They are older and don't like to get out more than they have to."

"Well, that isn't exactly true. They go on walks all the time, they just don't like to walk over here."

"Camellia," Charles warned.

His sister rolled her eyes at him. "It's true. The women are fit enough for their ages, they just like to play at being feeble when it is time to visit."

"Which reminds me," Charles said, his voice trailing off.

Camellia turned to him, eyebrows raised in curiosity. Then, she groaned. "It can't be time again. I do not want to go, Charles. They can't prepare a piece of toast between them, and they refuse to keep a cook. I could barely swallow whatever it was they served us last time."

"Some kind of wild game is my guess."

"Whatever it was, I swore I'd never let it touch my lips again," Camellia said, shaking her head. "I won't go."

I cleared my throat, drawing their attention to me. "I'm sorry, but you won't go where?"

Camellia smiled again, and I finally realized why the woman put me off. She smiled at me the way adults used to smile at me as a girl.

She tilted her head to the side and smiled as if I was a child playing dress up, and she had to indulge me.

Camellia was Charles' older sister, and Charles was several years older than Catherine, which meant Camellia had to be forty at least, though I would have placed her even older than that. Still, I did not deserve to be treated as a child simply because I was young, and I would make sure Camellia learned that lesson one way or another.

"To the Wilds' home for dinner," Camellia said. "They invite us to dinner once a week, at least, and it is always horrible. I've feigned illness the last few times—"

"Which only caused them to send along a horrid smelling soup to relieve you." Charles chuckled.

Camellia held her nose at the memory. "I think they foraged for the ingredients in the bogs. It smelled stagnant."

Charles smiled as he took another bite of roast, shaking his head. "They are thoughtful ladies, but unusual. Despite their eccentricities, they come from a good old family that has resided in this area for generations. If they live almost as if they are impoverished, it is their choice to do so."

"Sisters I take it, since they share a name?"

"Yes and unmarried," Camellia said. "They grew up in that house, inherited it from their parents, and have never lived anywhere else. Charles told me he never sees them go into the village for anything, and no one ever comes to visit them. We are their only source of outside interaction."

We.

It seemed strange that Camellia had joined herself together with her brother as a unit. She'd only been staying with Charles and Catherine for a couple of months, yet she had made herself quite comfortable in their world.

"Luckily, you won't have to deal with them once you return home," I said cheerfully.

All at once, the mood in the room shifted.

Every scrape of silverware against the plates was an explosion of sound, and the air felt like it had been pulled from the room. I'd meant for my words to make Camellia uncomfortable, but not like this. They'd had a much larger impact than I'd expected, and I wanted to know why.

"I'm sorry," I said, breaking the silence. "I'm not sure what I—"

"Camellia is free to stay as long as she likes," Charles said, interrupting me. "Catherine and I invited her here to live with us, and as long as she is pleased with the arrangement, so are we."

Camellia gazed downward at her plate, and I thought I saw her lip tremble.

"Of course. I didn't realize the situation was permanent. Excuse me if I offended."

"You're excused." Charles' tone was clipped, and left no room for further response.

I worried we would stay that way for the remainder of dinner until Charles cleared his throat and carried on the conversation as if nothing had happened at all.

"Margaret and Abigail sent an invitation for dinner this afternoon, and since Camellia is refusing to see them, I thought maybe you would like to accompany me, Alice?"

"What of Catherine?" I asked.

"Nurse Gray says she isn't ready for visiting," Camellia said.

I kept my eyes on Charles, watching his response. Surely, he would have something to say on behalf of his wife. And surely, he would rather be visiting neighbors with her than with his sister-in-law.

But Charles said nothing. He continued to eat and, after a little while, looked up at me. "So, Alice? Would you like to come?"

I wanted to refuse him and stay by my sister's side, but I also thought some time alone with Charles could be beneficial. Perhaps, away from the distressing atmosphere of the house, I could talk some sense into him. I could help him see that he was deserting his family to the control of outside forces, and it was high time he returned as the head of his household.

"Of course, Charles. If the lady of the house cannot go with you, then I would be happy to make the visit."

"It isn't that I cannot go," Camellia said. "But rather that I would prefer to do anything else."

Charles winced, and I stared at Camellia in awe, momentarily struck silent by the audacity of her words.

"I'm sorry, but I was speaking of my sister."

Camellia's mouth fell open, and she blinked several times before shaking her head. "Of course. I misheard you. Yes, of course."

Once again, the air left the room, and our awkward trio finished dinner in perfect silence.

6

I couldn't get in to see Catherine for the entirety of the next day.

"Nurse Gray isn't allowing anyone in," I said, standing in Charles' doorway.

He didn't look up from the letter he was writing as he answered. "Sometimes Catherine has better days than others. She had a nightmare last night, so today she is—"

"Incapable of speaking?" I asked. "I don't understand what that has to do with her being able to leave her room, Charles. None of this is making any sense to me. What is going on?"

"Confused," he said, setting down his pen and standing up. "Catherine is confused and it is hard to see her that way. So, Nurse Gray is tending to her in private."

I tried to argue, but Charles ushered me from the room under the pretense of writing an important letter and did not open the door again until it was time to leave for dinner.

Camellia met us in the entryway, holding out a hat for Charles as we neared the door. "Enjoy your time."

"You know we won't," Charles said with a smile.

Camellia wrinkled her nose and then turned to me, her smile slipping into a frown. I had not received a warm welcome from Hazel's other aunt, and I did not think her feelings would change anytime soon. "Steer clear of the tea."

"Thank you for the warning."

With that, we climbed into the car and set off for the home of Margaret and Abigail Wilds.

The conversation from dinner the night before had prepared me slightly for what to expect, but I wasn't sure any description could have done the Wilds sisters justice. Despite having the time and leisure all day to imagine what they would be like, I hadn't even come close to the bizarre reality.

The ladies, it appeared, were doing their very best to live up to their name.

The house, a crumbling two-story brick home, must have been impressive once but now it looked ancient and neglected. Vines wove themselves between the bricks, leaving long cracks in the foundation of the home, some of which stretched nearly from the ground to the roof line. It appeared to me that one strong wind would blow the entire place over.

Pulling up to Catherine and Charles' home the day before, I'd wondered whether they had a grounds person to keep up with the weeds and flower beds. I did not have to wonder such a thing with the Wilds' home. It was quite apparent no one kept up with the grounds at all. The inhabitants' method was to allow nature to reclaim what had always belonged to it. In a matter of years, the house would disappear into the moors.

"The inside is better," Charles said, answering my unspoken question. "The Wilds live a contrary life, but they are nice people."

"I'm sure," I said, not sure of anything at all. "Shall we go in?"

Charles parked the car in the middle of the garden because there was no obvious driveway. He said the women didn't own a car because they did not need one. I didn't know how that could be possible, but before I could ask, the front door of the house opened.

For a second, there was only the dark doorway—the interior of the house plunged deep into shadow. Then, a woman stepped forward.

Followed by another.

The two women could have been mirror images of one another. They were both tall and thin, their frames draped in layers of fabric that had been patched and stitched together with an untrained hand. Having spent very little time practicing my embroidery skills, I still felt I could have done a much better job with the garments. Though, the uneven stitches were hardly the most important thing I noticed.

The women wore no shoes.

Or stockings.

They greeted us outside in their bare feet, and I looked down several times to confirm I was truly seeing what I thought I was seeing.

"Alice?" One of the women asked, dispelling my brief impression that the pair might be servants, rather than the ladies of the house. The speaker's face split into a wide smile. She had tanned skin with wrinkles around the eyes and mouth, but she looked younger than I expected. Closer to my mother's age, whereas I thought they would be elderly women. "Charles said you would be coming to visit. We are so glad to finally meet you."

"You look nothing like your sister." The second woman stepped forward, her mouth pulled into a flat line.

"What Abigail means," the first woman said, narrowing her eyes at her sister, "is that it is rare for sisters to look so different from one another, yet be extraordinarily beautiful in their own ways."

"That makes you Margaret?" I asked with a smile.

The woman nodded, her curly white hair bouncing. Wooden clips held her hair down in the front, but the strands sprang back up immediately, creating a halo of hair around her head. Both sisters had the same hair. And the same clothes. And the same bare feet.

"Yes, forgive me." Charles jumped forward, took Margaret's hand and bowed slightly. "This is Margaret Wilds and Abigail Wilds," he said, pointing to the more serious sister standing closer to the doorway. "Our favorite neighbors."

"Their only neighbors," Margaret said. She stepped aside and waved us in. I didn't even bother looking around anymore for a housemaid.

Life on the moors was much different than I expected it would be.

The rooms were clean, but cluttered. Pieces of painted wood and pictures covered the walls, piles of rocks filled the shelves and decorated the centers of tables, and hand-woven rugs covered the floors, creating a patchwork of colors and materials and patterns. A large fire roared in the stone fireplace, but it had a utilitarian purpose, as well. A large pot hung over the flame, and I could hear something inside of it bubbling.

"Welcome to our home," Margaret said, coming from the dining room with a tarnished silver tray in her hands. A tea kettle and four mugs rattled on it. "I'm sure Charles prepared you for what it would be like to join us for dinner, but we hope you aren't overwhelmed by our customs. My sister and I like to live simply and do things the old ways."

I shook my head. "Not at all. Charles mentioned that you run your home differently, but he had only the best things to say about you."

She set the tea on a low table in front of a sofa covered in blankets and throws, and Charles' leg brushed against mine as he sat down. When I looked over, he was smiling and gladly accepting a cup of tea, but I could see the tension at the corners of his mouth. It had been a warning. Or rather, a reminder. *Steer clear of the tea.*

I accepted my cup and then took a cue from Charles who kept his cup in his lap, never once taking a drink.

"Others are not as kind to myself and my sister," Abigail said, taking a long, loud sip of her tea. "We have been ostracized from our nearest neighbors for years."

"I'm sorry. That must be unpleasant."

"Not especially," Abigail said. "I quite like the quiet."

Margaret chuckled. "My sister tends towards reclusiveness, but I like company. We were delighted when Catherine and Charles first came to see us. So delighted I'm afraid we frightened Catherine away. She never has come back for a visit."

"Not at all," Charles said. "Catherine tends towards reclusiveness, as well. When I come to visit you both, it leaves her time to be alone in the house. Anyway, the pregnancy and the baby...it is a lot for her to manage."

I tried to school my features into a neutral expression, but it was difficult when everything Charles was saying was patently false.

Catherine loved company. She enjoyed conversation, and even though the Wilds would no doubt disturb Catherine with their style of living, she would find it fascinating enough to come back and experience again and again. I'd only been there fifteen minutes and was already anxious for my next visit.

Also, Catherine hadn't been busy with Hazel at all. Not since Camellia Cresswell had arrived, anyway.

"Is Camellia still staying with you?" Abigail asked, as if reading my mind. There was something strange about the way she said the woman's name—a subtle sharpness to her voice that made me wonder whether she had noticed the same overbearing tendencies I had in my short time spent with the family thus far.

Charles feigned a drink of his tea, the murky liquid never slipping over the rim of his cup, and nodded. "Yes. I suspect she will be with us for some time."

"Sad story." Margaret shook her head and then released a long sigh. She picked up the conversation again before I could guess at what she meant. "Be sure to tell Catherine we would be delighted to have her as our guest again as soon as she feels up to it."

"She feels fine," Charles said quickly. "But I will pass the message along."

Margaret's eyes narrowed on Charles for a moment

before she rose to her feet and went to stir the bubbling liquid in the pot.

"My sister and I were lucky enough to trap two rabbits yesterday afternoon. That meat paired with mushrooms and herbs from our garden made the stew for our dinner." She wafted the steam from the pot up to her nose and smiled. "It should be ready shortly."

"I made bread." Abigail pointed to a wooden cutting board sitting on the side table. A dense loaf of bread with several slices sawed away sat on top of it.

"You are both very...resourceful," I said, finally landing on the correct word.

"People have done for themselves for centuries, and my sister and I see no need to rely on anyone else now," Margaret said, reclaiming her seat on the chair to my right. She crossed her ankles, and if it hadn't been for the wild state of her hair and dress, she would have looked like a proper lady. Her spine was tall and straight, shoulders pushed back and broad, chin lifted. She had enviable posture that even I couldn't emulate most of the time.

"I think it is admirable," Charles said. "Living from the land is a lost art."

I wasn't the only one who raised an eyebrow at my brother-in-law. As a recent transplant to the country life, he still looked much more suited to the fast-paced life of the city than one of working the land. Though he may have genuinely admired the Wilds—I suspected he didn't admire them as much as he claimed—I could not imagine Charles Cresswell fending for himself.

"You don't go into town for any supplies?" I asked.

Abigail shook her head, her jaw set. "Rarely. Between

the vegetable garden and our foraging, we have everything we need."

"We also have several people kind enough to give us discarded items that we can repurpose," Margaret explained. "Charles and Catherine are two such people."

"Our house was full of the previous owner's belongings," Charles explained. "It was nothing to give them to you for whatever you may need. Truly, it was a favor to us. You saved me having to dispose of them myself."

"No, it was very kind," Margaret insisted. "After waiting a few days so we could perform a cleansing ceremony under the full moon, we've used the tea cups every day since."

Margaret lifted her teacup into the air to show it off, but I couldn't pay any attention to the painted flowers around the rim of the cup. My mind had caught on another detail.

"Cleansing ceremony?" I asked, looking from the Wilds to Charles.

Charles pressed his lips together, his nostrils flaring in barely disguised frustration. Otherwise, he didn't move.

Margaret and Abigail, however, moved in closer. Each of the sisters sat up in their chairs and leaned in.

Margaret said, "The previous owner died in the house, so the items had to be cleansed. We have enough ghosts of our own without bringing in another."

Abigail nodded, clearly in agreement with her sister's every word.

"You believe in ghosts?" There didn't seem to be any way to ask the question without it sounding insulting, but it had to be asked. I needed a definitive answer.

Margaret set her cup down on the saucer and looked me in the eyes. "Absolutely, don't you?"

At that, I turned to Charles. He was sitting perfectly still, refusing to look towards me and meet my gaze, and I knew why.

His wife was currently locked away in her room at their house because she thought she'd seen a ghost. She was being forced to sleep multiple times a day and secluded because she believed she'd been attacked. All the while, he was visiting his eccentric neighbors for dinner who, it so happened, also believed in ghosts.

The irony could not be downplayed, and I felt my face growing hot with anger.

Whether Catherine truly was insane or not no longer mattered because, worse than being insane, Charles Cresswell was a hypocrite.

The stew began to bubble in earnest, and Margaret left to tend to it. Abigail went to slice more bread, grunting as her knife slowly worked through the loaf.

Charles and I were momentarily alone.

"They believe in ghosts," I whispered.

"It isn't the same thing, Alice," Charles hissed back. "They are old superstitious women. They live on the moors alone and have survived this way for decades. You and I both know Catherine is not like them."

"So you think they are mad, too?" I asked, shifting towards him, eyes narrowed. "If so, I'm not sure why we are here. Catherine has been deemed too dangerous to even be near her child."

His cheeks went red. "No one has said that. Catherine can see Hazel whenever she wishes."

"Whenever your sister allows it."

Finally, Charles looked at me, and I flinched away from the anger in his eyes. "Do not judge me, Alice. You've only been here one day. You don't know what it has been like. I allowed Catherine to invite you here because I thought you would help, but if you make things worse for Catherine and upset her, I'll happily take you back to the train station and send you home."

"You *allowed* Catherine to invite me here?" I asked, raising an eyebrow. "Did Catherine allow you to invite Camellia or did you make that decision yourself?"

"You don't understand that situation, either."

Abigail shifted slightly and looked back at us over her shoulder. Charles smiled at her, though it was obviously forced, and then leaned in closer to me, his voice low. "We can talk about this another time."

"We will," I assured him.

DINNER WAS SO MUCH WORSE than I expected.

I'd eaten rabbit meat plenty of times before, but I didn't recognize the meat in Margaret's stew as belonging to a rabbit. Or any other earthly creature, for that matter.

Biting into it felt like taking a bite out of a brick, and swallowing it was even worse. The meat was so dry it leeched moisture from my throat. I became so desperate for liquid that I took a sip of the tea Camellia had warned me against just to try and force the meat down my throat.

Unfortunately, her warnings were not for nothing.

The sludge inside of my teacup could barely be called tea. On first look, it sloshed around the cup like liquid, but once I tipped it into my mouth, the sediment at the bottom of the cup revealed itself and a thick brown slime dripped down my throat. I had to disguise my gag as a cough.

Despite our earlier argument, Charles reached over and patted me on the back.

"Are you all right, Miss Beckingham?" Margaret asked.

"Eating too quickly," I choked out. "The stew is wonderful."

Margaret smiled in a self-satisfied way, and I knew without a doubt that she believed my compliment to be sincere. If believing ghosts could haunt teacups was not a sign of insanity, then believing this stew to not only be edible, but delicious, certainly was.

I forced down a few spoonfuls of broth and a few cuts of crunchy carrot before I sat away from the table, hands over my stomach to show how full I was. In reality, I hoped the sound of my stomach growling wouldn't catch their attention.

"If you don't mind me asking, I'd like to know more about the ghosts you mentioned before."

Charles stiffened next to me, but I ignored him. I cared little about his opinion now.

"Oh, you are in no danger of being haunted, Alice. My sister and I routinely cleanse the house." Abigail's eyes were wide and sincere. The woman was much more subdued than her sister—more solemn—but I could tell she did care about my comfort. She didn't want me to be frightened. Of her or the ghosts.

"I believe you," I assured her. "But you mentioned that you both have enough spirits already without adding more. What did you mean by that? If you cleanse the house, then how do any spirits remain here?"

Abigail and Margaret shared a look—one I recognized as saying more than Charles or I was aware of—and then Margaret laid down her spoon and smiled at me. "There are some spirits we don't wish to be rid of."

I frowned. "I don't understand."

"Family," Abigail explained. "Members of our family who lived on this land before us. This property has been passed through the Wilds family for over a century, and my sister and I feel that it is no place of ours to expel our relatives from their home."

"If this is where they wish to make their eternal rest, then we will cohabitate with them." Margaret lifted her arms into the air, gesturing around the room as though I should be able to look around and see her family members sitting amongst us.

There was, of course, no one but the four of us.

"How exactly do you cleanse spirits that are not members of your family? And how do other spirits come to live here?"

Abigail folded her hands in front of her, and I noticed how calloused and scarred they were. She had spent much of her life using them for manual labor. Whatever I thought about their life out here on the moors, they were devoted to it.

"Sometimes spirits come with a person," she said. "Like Nurse Gray. She only stayed with us for a brief time, but she came with a whole host of spirits. I suppose it can be expected, working in the field of medicine."

"Nurse Gray stayed with you?"

"Margaret and Abigail recommended Nurse Gray to

me when Catherine..." Charles' voice tapered off before picking back up again. "When we needed the assistance."

Margaret tipped her head at Charles in acknowledgement and turned back to me. "Sometimes we see Nurse Gray on her daily walks when we are out as well to gather bones."

I turned towards Abigail. "Excuse me?"

"On the moors," Margaret continued. "We walk the trails and scavenge for animal remains and ancient human remains. They are a direct link to the spirit of each creature and they allow us to connect with them."

Charles sighed next to me, drawing Abigail's attention. Once he knew he had one of the Wilds' eyes on him, he took a hasty spoonful of soup and smacked his lips together, feigning enjoyment.

"It is a hobby more than a necessity, but we enjoy it," Margaret said.

Soon after this conversation, Charles stood up, thanked our hosts for having us, and insisted we had to get home before dessert could be served. I, for one, was quite curious what would constitute a dessert in the Wilds home, but they did not press us to stay.

Margaret, however, did stop me at the door.

"Please come back again and see us before you leave," she said, grabbing my arm. "We would love the company. It isn't often we meet people who are curious about our life and ways."

I laid my hand over hers. "Gladly. I'll come so often you'll be weary of me."

I couldn't explain my fondness for the strange women. They should have frightened me. Their way of living and interests were bizarre and unsettling. But

Margaret and Abigail Wilds were authentic. They were truly themselves despite it all, and being around them felt refreshing. It held a larger appeal than remaining in my sister's home where everyone seemed to have some kind of ulterior motive.

Charles didn't speak to me until we were at the end of the drive and turning onto the road back to his own home, almost as though he thought the Wilds had the ability to hear him wherever he was on their property.

"What the Wilds do is different, Alice."

I crossed my arms over my chest. "I don't see how."

"They are old ladies living in an isolated area who cure their loneliness with spirits. I allow them onto our property for daily walks. They say they are coming to look for bones, but I know they like being near other people after a lifetime spent alone in that crumbling house." Charles shook his head. "All of their claims of ghosts and spirits come back to one thing: they want for human connection. Catherine already has that."

I turned to my brother-in-law. His face was tinged with color from the headlights, but otherwise, he was in the dark. I could see that he believed what he was saying. It showed in the set of his jaw and the press of his lips.

But I could also see the tiny flicker of doubt in his eyes, and I hoped to fan that flicker into a flame.

"Do you truly believe that, Charles?" I asked quietly. "Alone in that room, sleeping her days away. Does she really? Because I don't think so."

7

W hen I came down to breakfast the next morning and saw Catherine at the table, I hoped my conversation with Charles the night before had been effective. I hoped he'd seen the error of his ways and decided to allow his wife more freedoms. It wasn't fair that Catherine should be locked away for the same reasons the Wilds were interesting neighbors. I hadn't seen her do anything dangerous since my arrival, and if anything, being around people would only improve her condition.

As soon as Charles walked into the room, however, my hopes were dashed.

His eyes widened at the sight of Catherine sitting to the right of the head chair, and he crossed the room briskly, never letting his eyes waver from her.

"Did Nurse Gray permit you to come down to breakfast?" he asked quietly, a hand on her shoulder.

Catherine's cheeks heated with embarrassment, but she smiled through it. "I do not need permission to eat breakfast in my own home, Charles. I came down by my own choice. As you can see, I'm fine."

Unlike the first day I'd arrived, Catherine had changed out of her nightgown. She wore a cotton dress that hugged her wider hips, and her long hair was twisted back into a loose bun at the nape of her neck. She didn't look exactly like the sister I remembered, but she looked more like her than she had two days ago, and that seemed like something to celebrate.

"Indeed," I agreed. "You look wonderful this morning, Catherine. Perhaps we should take another walk. It seemed to do you good the other day."

Catherine gave me a warm smile in appreciation, but it faded away just as Camellia Cresswell entered the room with a gasp.

"Catherine," she said, placing a hand over her chest in feigned shock. "I didn't expect you to join us this morning."

"It is my house," Catherine reminded her coolly. "I'm not sure why everyone is so shocked."

I couldn't remember Catherine talking much about her feelings towards Camellia. She'd mentioned that Camellia was the one who suggested keeping Catherine from Hazel until they could be certain she wouldn't be a danger to her own baby, but most of her frustration had seemed to be aimed at Charles and Nurse Gray. Now, however, I could see the anger.

Catherine felt threatened by Camellia, and I didn't think her feelings were misplaced. Camellia needed to be set straight. She, like myself, was a guest in Catherine's home, and it couldn't hurt to remind her of that.

"Regardless, it is lovely to have you." Camellia smiled,

but it looked more like a grimace, the emotion not reaching her eyes. As she took her seat opposite Catherine—but still next to Charles—she waved to the maid.

The young woman had been going back and forth to the kitchen all morning bringing in the food one item at a time. Usually, the kitchen staff would have brought out the food all at once, but it seemed the girl was working alone. I was so uncomfortable waiting for her to pour everyone a glass of juice that I considered offering to help.

Camellia made a motion to her.

"Yes?" The maid's eyes flicked to Catherine's briefly as she lowered her head. Even the staff sensed the shifting of the power dynamic.

"Be sure to take something up to the nanny," Camellia instructed, sweeping a hand across her forehead, her eyes fluttering closed dramatically. "Hazel was awake most of the night, and the poor woman could use something to revive her. I know I certainly could."

Catherine's brows knit together, and she turned to Charles. "Is Hazel all right? Why wasn't I told?"

Camellia waved away Catherine's concern with a laugh. "It is just her age. She needs to be soothed several times a night, and she is so hungry. Growing every day."

At that, I frowned. Hazel was young enough that she should be eating only from her mother. Was Camellia feeding her something else? Since Catherine was taking medicine and spent so much of her time napping in her room, perhaps they had made other arrangements?

It looked as though Catherine wanted to ask something, as well, but doing so would be admitting that she didn't have a say in the parenting of her own child. As much as I wanted to know the answer, I understood her silence on the subject.

"Did you drink the tea?" Camellia asked, looking up at me from beneath her dark brows.

For a moment, I didn't know what she was referring to. Then, I remembered the Wilds. "Oh, yes. Unfortunately. Only to help me swallow the stew."

"Oh no. They served the stew?" Camellia wrinkled her nose and grabbed her brother's wrist. "Did you eat it, too, Charles?"

"Only the broth when they were looking directly at me. It was rabbit again."

"You went to visit Margaret and Abigail?" Catherine asked.

Charles looked up for only a second, barely catching her eye. "Alice and I went last night."

My sister turned to me, a look of betrayal on her face.

I would have spoken to Catherine about it directly if it hadn't been for Nurse Gray's rules. I hadn't been able to see my sister the entire day before the dinner, and Charles led me to believe Catherine knew about it.

In turn, I looked at my brother-in-law with the same expression. Wisely, Charles kept his head down, avoiding my ire.

"Margaret and Abigail both had favorable things to say about you, Cat." I forced a smile. "They told me to visit them again. Perhaps you could come with me and—"

"No." Catherine lifted her chin and cut into the berries on her plate, bright red and purple juices spreading across the china, soaking into the bread.

I waited for more of an explanation, but none came. Finally, I pressed. "If it is because of the distance, the drive there is quite short. I'm sure Charles wouldn't mind escorting us, and—"

"No thank you, Alice. You go on ahead."

"Catherine," I argued. "The tea truly is horrible, but the women are lovely, and I think it could be good for you to—"

"No!" Catherine's fork slipped from her grip, clattering against her plate and falling to the floor.

Camellia gasped, a melodramatic hand flying over her mouth, and Charles stilled. He became an immovable statue, neither addressing his wife's outburst or carrying on as though it hadn't happened. Instead, he stayed fixed in that moment, staring down at his place, fork hovering over a pile of scrambled eggs.

Catherine smoothed her hands down the front of her dress and scooted her chair away from the table to retrieve her fork. When she sat back up, her face was pale.

"Perhaps I do need to rest," she said softly, her voice barely above a whisper. "I'm sorry. I just—"

She got up to leave and tripped over the leg of a chair, catching herself on the back of my chair to keep from falling.

"Catherine, I'm sorry," I started. "Do you want me to help you—"

"I'm fine, Alice." She laid her hand on my shoulder, and her fingers were cold. The chill seeped beneath my blouse and sunk into my skin. She summoned a small smile on her way out of the room. "Perhaps we can go on that walk later. I would like that."

"All right, Cat."

I didn't know what happened, and when Catherine left, no one seemed keen to discuss it. Camellia went on about Hazel's night-time habits and how big she was growing, and Charles just nodded along absently.

I wondered if he was worried about his wife. It seemed like he was, but his actions didn't show it. More than anything, it seemed like Charles wanted someone else to solve his problems.

Unfortunately, it seemed as though that person would have to be me.

WHEN I WENT up to see Catherine later in the afternoon, Nurse Gray opened the door.

She had on the same dark dress as the day before—or, if not the same one, then one very similar—and her hair was pulled back into a tight bun. She folded her hands behind her back, blocking the door.

"Mrs. Cresswell is sleeping."

I angled myself to look around her, trying to see my sister, but Nurse Gray pulled the door partway closed. "She is tired and needs her rest."

"She told me she wanted to go on a walk this afternoon," I said. "She requested that I come find her when I was ready to go."

This wasn't entirely true, but I hoped, if nothing else, Catherine's own wishes would sway Nurse Gray's iron will.

Unfortunately, they did nothing to sway the nurse.

"I'm sorry, but today has been tiring for her. Perhaps, you can try again tomorrow."

Before I could formulate a better argument or desperately shout into the room to try and rouse Catherine from her unnatural sleep, the door closed, and I was alone in the hallway.

Camellia had, once again, been in the nursery with Hazel all morning, and Charles had gone into town.

The house was quiet and eerie, and I couldn't stay inside for another minute. So, I pulled on a coat and set off on a walk.

Not wanting to trudge through the bogs along the trails or be submerged in shadow under the trees, I walked down the driveway towards the road rather than following the paths behind the house. Once I reached the road, I turned left, and it was only when I turned left again on the Wilds' property that I realized where my feet were actually carrying me.

Margaret and Abigail must have seen me coming because they were in the yard when I crested the final hill in front of their house.

Abigail had a hand raised to her eyes, squinting against the gray light in the overcast sky, and Margaret was plucking handfuls of weeds from the garden in front of their house. They'd built wire cages around the produce, probably to keep smaller animals from getting to the food. On a hook near the corner of the house, I noticed one such small animal hanging by its foot. Its lifeless body swayed in the wind.

If the women offered me stew today, I would decline. I did not want rabbit again.

"I hope you don't mind me coming by unannounced," I called once I was close enough.

"Of course, not," Margaret responded, wiping her dirty hands on the sides of her dress, leaving streaks of dirt on the brown fabric. "Like we said, you are always welcome at our home."

My mother would have been horrified by my lack of manners, but she also would have been horrified by Margaret and Abigail Wilds, so I didn't think it mattered much. Besides, if what Charles had said the night before was true—that the Wilds were lonely—then they really wouldn't mind my surprise visit.

"We are making preserves today. If you don't mind helping, then you can stay as long as you like." Abigail held out a cloth sack full of bruised apples.

"She doesn't have to help." Margaret chastised her sister and then turned to me, shaking her head. "You don't have to help, Alice. We are just happy for the company."

I didn't mind the work. It was much better than staying in my sister's quiet home. Besides, even though I hadn't consciously planned to come visit the Wilds, I was glad for the opportunity to talk with them without Charles present. I had some questions.

The women had at least six apple trees behind their house. As we picked up the apples from the ground, Margaret told me they had been a gift to their father when they were only girls.

"He helped the previous owner of your sister's home deliver a newborn calf. The man was poor, but he had a hearty garden, and he uprooted several of his own trees and strapped them to his horse, hauling them here one by one. Father didn't think they would last the season, but sixty years later, here they are."

"I propogated the three in the back from the one on the right," Abigail said. "That was almost twenty years ago now. The children grow sweeter apples than their mother."

"But the mother's are the best for pie," Margaret said.

Abigail nodded in agreement. "Tart apples make the best pie."

The trees all looked identical to me, but the women knew them all intimately. It made sense. If they had as few visitors as they claimed, then this land—these trees and this garden—were their entire life. These trees were a kind of family to them.

"We lost one tree during a particularly dry spring and a harsh summer. It became diseased, and we had to pull it up by the root to keep it from infecting the others." Abigail turned towards the house and pointed at a large stone with an apple carved into it. The stone had a wide bottom and came to a narrow point at the top, much like the stone Charles had laid at the base of the pathway behind his house. "We buried it there."

"You buried the tree?"

Margaret hummed in assent. "We burned the wood in the fireplace and scraped out the ashes. The tree's ashes deserved to be back in the ground."

"So, you gave it a funeral?"

"Exactly." Margaret smiled. "Every living thing deserves to be celebrated."

"And if we didn't, there was a chance the other trees would fall to the same illness," Abigail added.

If anyone else had made that claim, I would have

assumed it had something to do with the disease and the proximity to the other trees—something scientific. But with the Wilds, I suspected the women were worried about a curse from a vengeful tree spirit.

"I'm sorry, but I have to ask—"

"Ask us anything." Margaret smiled.

I dropped several more apples into my bag and then let it slide from my shoulder to the ground. My arms ached from the work. Unlike Margaret and Abigail, I wasn't accustomed to physical labor. I rolled my shoulder and took a deep breath. "You said people can carry spirits with them...so, I wonder whether...well, if you've noticed any spirits attached to me?"

Margaret set her apple bag on the ground. Her cheeks and nose were red from the cold, and she rubbed her hands together to spread some warmth in them. "Are you worried about that, Alice? Because if so, I can tell you there is nothing malicious around you at all. If there had been, we wouldn't have let you into the house."

"Or onto the property," Abigail said over her shoulder, still picking up fallen apples. "We don't allow evil spirits into our home if we can stop them."

"I'm not afraid. Only curious." The breeze picked up and a chill slid down my spine, spreading goosebumps across my arms. "I've...experienced death before. I just wonder—"

"Catherine told us about your brother."

I snapped my attention up to Margaret and frowned. "She did?"

The woman nodded. Her white hair blew freely in the wind, and she looked more like a spirit herself than a human being. True to their surname, there was something wild about the two sisters. Something untethered.

After the way Catherine had reacted to my offer of joining me to visit the women, I was surprised to learn she'd divulged anything personal to them at all.

"When she first came to visit, I told her I sensed a ghost following her," Abigail said, walking over to stand behind her own sister, a bag of apples hanging from each elbow. "She seemed uncomfortable, and I'm afraid we may have frightened her with such talk."

Last night I would have assured the women that wasn't the case. But after the way Catherine became so upset this morning, I couldn't be sure.

Once all of the apples were gathered, we took the bags inside and dropped them on the kitchen table. The same pot from the night before was boiling in the fireplace, and I was worried I'd have to try and stomach more of Margaret's stew, but when I walked over to the fire to warm up, I could smell the sweetness. It was sugar syrup for the apples. One of the cooks we had growing up had let me help her preserve fruits once before. I couldn't remember her name, but I remembered stealing bites of the fruit when the woman's back was turned.

Abigail handed me a knife, handle first, and we all sat down at the table with a bag of apples on one side and a bowl on the other. We peeled, cored, and sliced the apples, being sure to save the scraps to be composted for the garden.

"You never actually answered my question," I said after a particularly long stretch of silence.

"Huh?" Margaret asked, tongue between her teeth while she focused on peeling her apple in one cut. She and Abigail had been challenging each other to see who could have the longest unbroken stretch of peel. My attempts were laughable, but Abigail had nearly peeled an entire apple without lifting her knife once.

"Are there any spirits attached to me?"

Both women set down their apples immediately, their competition forgotten, and looked at me. Their attention made my neck tingle, and I lowered my knife, too.

"You aren't as open to it as your sister," Margaret said. "You are a charming young woman, but your energy is suspicious."

"There is nothing wrong with that," Abigail cut in.

"Especially since Abigail is the same way," Margaret smiled, pointing a thumb towards her sister. "No, there is nothing wrong with being hesitant. It is wise. But it does not mean you are safe. There are shadows around you. Vague and hazy, but present."

I looked around my head, feeling foolish. "Do you mean actual shadows?"

"No, but wouldn't it be nice if it were that easy?" Margaret laughed.

"It just means you have been touched by death." Abigail pressed a finger to her chest, just above her heart. "Here."

Before I could get a grip on my emotions, moisture sprang to my eyes. Immediately, I blinked away the tears and went back to peeling my apples. A few moments later, the Wilds did the same.

Once I had my emotions under control, I asked the other question that had been weighing heavily on my mind. "You two knew Nurse Gray before she came to work for my sister and brother-in-law, correct?"

"Right," Margaret said, laying down her stretch of peel next to Abigail's and wrinkling her nose in disappointment when it was a few finger widths short. "It was many years ago when she was still only a midwife."

I frowned, and Margaret understood my confusion before I could even voice the question. "Neither of us have children, but our sister did."

"There were once three of us," Abigail added. "Dorothea was the youngest."

Apple peeling forgotten, I leaned forward onto my elbows. "What happened to her?"

Margaret opened her mouth to answer, but Abigail cut her off. "She died. Nurse Gray was tending to her before it happened. We recommended her to Charles before Catherine even gave birth in case he would need to call on a nurse. Luckily, she has been able to be there for Catherine while she has been ill."

"How is Catherine doing?" Margaret asked. "Charles doesn't talk about her much, and we don't want to press."

"Catherine is..." I didn't know how to answer. I could lie, which was what Charles, and maybe even Catherine, would want me to do, but I wanted to reveal the truth. If only so I could ask the Wilds outright whether Nurse Gray could be trusted. In the end, I settled on an answer similar to the one Charles had given me. "Catherine is doing physically well."

"Good, good," Margaret breathed, nodding. "When we found her out on the moors, I couldn't believe it was her. She was covered in mud and blood and...it was a horrible sight."

The information took a few seconds to settle over me.

I froze, repeating the words in my mind to be sure I'd understood. "You found Catherine?"

"Did you not know that?" Abigail held her apple bowl under the rim of the table and swiped a large pile of apples into it with her forearm. "This time of year, the astronomical alignment brings us closer to the ghostly realm than any other time, so we are often out on the moors."

"In fact, there is a full moon coming later this week. Sunday, I believe," Margaret added.

Abigail nodded in agreement and continued. "Catherine had been out there for an hour or more by the time we found her. Luckily, it wasn't as cold as it is now."

"Charles would have found her if we hadn't," Margaret said. "By the time we got Catherine to the house, he'd already been growing nervous and was restless to go and find her."

Abigail stood up and walked around the table, dumping all of the apple slices into one large pot, while Margaret brought out a woven basket full of mismatched glass jars with different lids. Abigail motioned for me to stand and join them at the end of the table, and she showed me how to fill a jar with apple slices. When I was done with the first one, I slid the jar to Margaret, who ladled in hot sugar syrup to cover the apples.

My mind worked as quickly as my hands.

Catherine claimed to see spirits and to have been attacked by a ghost while, next door, her neighbors believed they communicated with the dead. It seemed too strange to be a coincidence, which led me to believe it wasn't.

Maybe one visit to the Wilds' home had been enough

to make Catherine paranoid and convince her that ghosts existed and she was surrounded by them.

"Screw the lids on as tight as you can," Abigail instructed for the third time. Once it became clear I was not paying attention to her commands, she sent me over to the fireplace to watch the jars boiling over the fire. The boiling water pressurized the jars, and when they were done, the metal lid popped up with a firm clicking sound. My only job was to pull the jars from the water once this was done.

The job was simple, and when Margaret and Abigail got into an argument about how high to fill the jars with apples, I let my mind wander.

I stepped away from the hearth and studied the shelves and picture frames that hung on the walls of the crumbling house. Much like everything else in the home, the shelves and frames needed a good dusting, but they gave me a look into exactly how eccentric the two women really were.

Small picture frames were filled with hand drawings of the moon and its different cycles, portraits of the sisters with colorful auras painted around their heads, and bits of poetry written out in ink that spoke of nature. One of them I recognized. It was a poem by Robert Frost. I remembered my mother fawning over him when he won some award when I was just a little girl. I still didn't have much of an appreciation for poetry, but it seemed the Wilds did. Every other part of their life was self-reliant and separate from society, except for their contemporary tastes in poetry.

The quartet was drawn in the center of a white piece of paper with hand-painted leaves falling from the branches of a tree and gathering on the ground. The quartet read:

> Then leaf subsides to leaf.
> So Eden sank to grief,
> So dawn goes down to day.
> Nothing gold can stay.

Just next to the poem in a matching frame was a formal portrait of a young woman.

When I first saw the picture, I shook my head, not understanding what I was looking at. The girl had long blonde hair that was pinned back over her ears, and the artist had given her piercing blue eyes. She had a pointed chin, rosy cheeks, and a sly smile pulled up to one side that made the viewer feel as though the woman knew a secret she had not revealed.

The woman in the picture, as far as I could tell, was my sister, Catherine.

I stepped back and opened my mouth to say something to Margaret and Abigail, to get some kind of explanation, when I looked at the bottom of the picture and saw the name written there: Dorothea.

The woman in the painting was Dorothea Wilds.

I could see now that the painting was yellowed with age and spotted from water damage. It was probably older than my sister, so therefore could not be her.

And yet...the likeness was shocking.

"Alice," Margaret said just over my shoulder.

I jumped, bumping into the woman. She grabbed my shoulders and steadied me.

"Sorry, dear, but the jars." She pointed to the fireplace, and I could hear a few of the lids popping up.

I rushed over and pulled them from the water with the tongs, but I didn't put any more into the water. I had other things to deal with.

"I'm sorry, but—" I pointed at the picture frame. "I saw this picture, and your sister looked so much like Catherine."

Abigail stiffened behind us where she was filling jars. Margaret frowned. "Does she?"

I looked at her, mouth agape. "Yes. They could be twins."

"I'm not sure I see it," Abigail said, wiping her sticky hands on a towel that was thrown over her shoulder.

"Maybe I can," Margaret said. "It has been so long since I've seen Catherine that I'm not sure, but perhaps."

"Perhaps?" I stared at the painting and shook my head. To me, the resemblance was exact.

"I actually think we can take the rest of the preserving from here," Abigail said, dropping new jars into the boiling water. "There isn't much else to do, and after this, us old women will likely go to bed."

I looked out the window and realized the sun was starting to sink below the horizon. I'd eaten so many apples while slicing them that I hadn't even thought about lunch, and now it was nearly time for dinner.

"I set out for a walk and never returned," I said, hurrying to grab my coat from the hook behind the door. "My sister will be worried about me. Thank you both so much for letting me help, but I really should be going."

"Of course," Margaret said, holding open the front door. "But please do come back anytime."

I made no promises and set out for the walk home.

By the time I made it back, the sky was dark. Charles looked surprised when I walked through the door. The rest of the house was business as usual. Catherine was asleep, Camellia and the nanny were in the nursery, and the rest of the household staff were going about their duties preparing dinner.

No one had realized I'd been gone at all.

8

Camellia didn't come down for dinner the night I came back from the Wilds' home, and she didn't join us for breakfast, either.

"Where is Camellia?" Catherine asked.

We had very little to talk about as a group since Charles wanted to avoid all conversation of Catherine's illness, Catherine wanted to avoid all conversation of the Wilds, and I wanted to talk about both of those things simultaneously.

I did not especially want to talk about Camellia, though.

She glared at me whenever we were in the same room, and I knew she was counting the days until I returned to London. That was not even a guess on my part. She had outright asked me when I would be returning so she could mark it on her calendar. When I told her I wasn't sure, she let out a forlorn sigh and then claimed it was because she hadn't slept much again due to Hazel's crying.

I, for one, never heard any crying in the night.

My room was on the opposite side of the hallway, but I would still have heard a baby crying.

"My sister is in the nursery, I think," Charles said.

Catherine's brow lifted slightly, and then she nodded. "She has been helping Molly a great deal with Hazel's care."

"She enjoys it. I think it helps her." Charles gave Catherine a knowing look that I did not understand.

As soon as breakfast was over, Catherine went back up to her room to rest, and I tried to stay in the sitting room and read. I tried to keep myself occupied and out of trouble. But life in the country was rather dull, and I had two options: walk the two miles to visit Margaret and Abigail Wilds again or stay at the house.

As much as the two women next door entertained me, there had been a strange energy there when I'd left the day before, and I did not want to overwhelm them with my company.

Anyway, I had things I needed to do in my sister's home.

Namely, speak with Charles.

My brother-in-law was stooped over a letter on his desk, his hand pressed to his forehead in concentration when I knocked on the door. He looked up, and I could see the disappointment on his face.

He and I had never been close.

Honestly, there hadn't been much opportunity for a relationship to form between us. When he'd first met Catherine in New York City, I was a young girl, hardly worth his time or energy. More than that, I hadn't wanted to know him. I'd been far too busy chasing after boys.

Then, he and Catherine got married and stayed in New York City while I lived with my parents in London. When they did return to England, they settled in Yorkshire, where I had only briefly visited them.

So, no, Charles and I were not friends by any stretch. But he was my sister's husband, and I needed to speak with him.

"I was hoping to talk with you for a few minutes."

He winced. "I'm actually rather busy. Do you think it could wait until—"

"Thanks, I'll come on in." I stepped into his study and pulled the door closed behind me.

"Alice," Charles warned, his tone deep and somber. "I'm starting to think this was all a mistake. Catherine wanted you here, but it seems like things are getting worse. I don't blame you by any means, but—"

"That is good," I said, interrupting him again. "Because none of this is my fault. It is yours."

Charles opened and closed his mouth several times, looking for the words to respond to me. Whatever he'd thought I wanted to talk about, he clearly didn't think I'd be so forthright. But based on what I'd seen going on in his house thus far, there wasn't time for anything less than brutal honesty.

"I'm sorry, but I've noticed some troubling things, and I have a hard time thinking you haven't noticed them, too."

"Of course, I've noticed," he snapped. "My wife is unwell. How could I not notice?"

I shook my head and dropped down into the chair opposite him. "It isn't just about Catherine. It's about the way this house is running. It's about...Nurse Gray keeping watch over Catherine like she is a prisoner. It is about your sister playing mother to your daughter. It is about you hiding away in this study and doing nothing to help any of it."

"Nothing?" Charles' eyes were wide, his pupils expanded and dark. An angry red leaked into his cheeks. "I feel like all I've done for months is worry about everyone around me, Alice. I'm barely eating or sleeping. I'm stretched as thin as I possibly can be, and it still isn't enough."

"Catherine isn't ill enough to warrant that kind of response," I started. "I'm not sure why you—"

"It's Camellia, too."

I frowned. "Camellia is unwell?"

"Something like it." Charles folded his hands on the desk in front of him and leaned forward, sagging in his chair. "She doesn't like to speak of it, and neither do I, honestly. I'm not a very emotional man, and I don't like to dwell on things I cannot fix. And I certainly cannot fix Camellia's problems."

I sat perfectly still and silent, desperate to know what he was going to say next.

Finally, Charles sighed. "Her husband and child died. One day after Hazel was born."

"No." I clapped a hand over my mouth and shook my head.

I'd asked Camellia whether she missed her family, and her response had been strange. At the time, I'd assumed she was painting herself as the victim of an ungrateful husband. Now, I knew better.

I'm afraid I miss them far more than they miss me.

"How did it happen?"

"A fire." Charles took a steadying breath and shook his head. "Camellia was pregnant for part of Catherine's pregnancy. She gave birth four months before Hazel was born. Though Camellia is older than me by several years, Grace was her first child. One conceived after many failures before. She was more precious to my sister than anything."

I felt tears pressing at the backs of my eyes. My opinion of Camellia had been so low since my arrival because of her surly demeanor and ownership over Hazel, but now it all made sense. Though it did not make her behavior acceptable, it did make it understandable.

"The day of the fire, Camellia left the house for a walk," he said. "It was the first time she'd left since having Grace. The baby wasn't sleeping well, and she cried for hours after eating, only to eat and have the cycle begin again. It was exhausting for them, as you can imagine, and Camellia wanted a break. So, she fed Grace, left her with George, and then went for a walk around town. She walked for almost two hours, stopping in at a few places to pick up another bonnet for Grace and cigars for George. Then, she headed home. She saw the smoke from the edge of town."

I pressed my hand over my mouth and closed my eyes.

"Neighbors were pouring water on the flames by the time the house came into view, but Camellia said it was like throwing pebbles at a dragon. The flames were so high they blotted out the sky. She couldn't see anything beyond them." Charles cleared his throat, fighting through his own emotion. "She searched the crowd for George and Grace, but every person she met told her that they were both still inside the house. 'What house?' she'd asked. The structure was just a crumbling wooden frame by that point. They found the bodies once the embers cooled."

It felt as though someone had hollowed my insides. I had never known George or Grace or seen the house where they lived, but it was all so clear in my mind. I imagined it like my parents house, large and stately, hidden behind a metal gate that would survive the blaze. I could see myself walking down the street, see the neighbors I'd grown up with gathered on the sidewalks. I could picture the stomach dropping horror that would overwhelm me when I saw the flames lashing out of windows and doors, devouring the life I'd known from the inside out.

"I can't imagine," I said, though I already was. "How is she doing?"

Charles leaned back in his chair and shrugged. "As good as can be expected. Being with Hazel helps her. It reminds her of Grace."

His comment to Catherine at breakfast that morning made more sense now. He'd been right. I did understand the dynamic of the house better. Though, to Charles' disappointment, I was sure, my understanding did not mean agreement.

"Is that a good thing, though?" I asked gently. It was now apparent I'd stepped into a situation without knowing all of the facts, and I would try not to bully my way into matters that didn't concern me, but this did concern me. Clearly, Catherine felt uncomfortable with her relationship with Hazel, which made this issue my highest concern. Especially since I believed wholeheartedly that solving the problems surrounding Hazel's care would help to heal my sister immensely. If 'heal' was the proper word. I still did not understand what it was she needed to be healed of, other than a possibly overactive imagination.

"Camellia feeling better isn't good?" Charles asked defensively.

"No. I mean, is it a good thing for her to be reminded of Grace in Hazel?" I tangled my fingers together and looked down at my lap, hoping I looked as humble as I felt. "Camellia's loss is greater than most people could ever imagine—more painful than almost anything a human can bear—and I'm not sure the solution should be to hand her another child."

Charles sat up, his neck strained, head cocked to the side. "I'm not *handing* anyone my child. I'm making sure she is cared for."

"I know Camellia is good with Hazel," I admitted. "They love each other, and that is wonderful, but I just wonder if it is a good situation for everyone in the house."

Charles pushed away from his desk and stood up, shoving his hands into his front pockets. Still, I could see they were fisted in frustration. "See here, Alice. I know you were brought here to help your sister, but I imagined you would speak with her and talk sense into her. I did not ask you here to question the way I am running my house."

"You aren't running your house!" The words were out of me before I could consider, and I regretted them immediately. I tried walking them back, but it was too late. They'd struck at Charles' center, as intended.

"Everyone in my care is in need of something," he

said, voice ominously steady. I'd rarely seen Charles in any burst of emotion, and the few times I had, he was in ecstasy. The day he and Catherine were engaged, at their wedding, when they announced they were expecting. Never before had I seen him livid. Until now. "My wife needs constant attention, as does my newborn daughter, and my sister is grieving a loss I cannot fully understand. So, if two of those people are able to care for one another in ways I can't, how am I supposed to refuse them one another?"

"You are Hazel's father. You can care for her better than anyone else who is not her parent."

"I can't nurse her," Charles snapped.

Wet nurses were not unheard of, especially when a mother was ill, but the confirmation that Camellia was nursing my sister's child as her own made me even more uneasy.

We sat in silence for a moment, letting the tensions in the room abate slightly. My intention was not to upset Charles, but to open his eyes to the possible issues with his current solution. He appeared to want to stand back and allow the women in his life to heal themselves, but I believed he would be better off with a more active approach.

He wanted me to speak sense to Catherine, but who could understand and appeal to her more than her husband? If he would try to understand where she was coming from, perhaps he would see she was not insane. And that she certainly did not need to be tended to by Nurse Gray, who seemed to want to do nothing more than send her into unconsciousness.

With Camellia, I did not have a perfect solution for

that, but I knew the hole in her heart could not be filled with another child. It needed to be mended with time and compassion.

"I see you are trying, and I appreciate that," I said softly. "You have always loved my sister well, and my family loves you for it. You know that. However—"

"Must there be a however, Alice? I'm tired, and I think—"

"However," I continued, holding up a hand for him to allow me to finish. "I just wonder whether Camellia is healed enough from her trauma to be trusted with Hazel's care?"

He narrowed his eyes. "Do you think my sister unwell?"

"Isn't she? Any person in her position would be unwell, don't you think?" I pressed a hand to my heart. "I do not have a husband or child to lose, but I've lost a brother. I've seen people die before my eyes, and...it is a wound not easily healed. I just worry what spending so much time with Hazel is doing to your sister. You would hate for her to become confused."

I saw Charles' face shift, his eyes go flat, shuttering themselves against any more of my appeals. He shook his head. "She is not confused. She is distracting herself from her troubles, and I do not think that is a bad thing. It does not do to dwell on situations like the one my sister endured. There is nothing to be done about it, so one might as well carry on as best as possible."

My brother-in-law walked around his desk and extended an arm, ready to lead me from the room. I remained in my chair, determined for my point to be heard.

"She cannot simply carry on. This isn't like a rainy day ruining a picnic, Charles. Your sister's family died in a horrible way, and she needs to deal with those feelings before she throws herself into mothering again."

"Thank you for your thoughts, Alice. I'll keep them in mind." He laid a hand on my shoulder and all but forced me from the chair. "But I need to attend to some business."

He ushered me towards the door, pulled it open, and I stopped short.

Standing just on the other side was Camellia.

I felt Charles stiffen next to me, and I went wide-eyed, not sure what to expect. Would she rage at me for doubting her ability to care for Hazel? Would she be angry with Charles for sharing such a personal part of her history with me? Had she overheard our conversation at all?

A second later, Camellia smiled and stood aside. "I'm sorry, I didn't know anyone was in here with you, brother. I can come back."

"No, no." I gave her a shaky smile and stepped aside. "Please, come in. I was just leaving. I think I'm going to go see my sister."

"She's sleeping." Camellia smiled so big her eyes crinkled at the corners, and I couldn't remember her ever looking so cheerful.

It looked forced.

"Maybe later, then." I nodded my head at the siblings and headed for the stairs, desperate to be alone in my own room.

As soon as I got there, I locked the door behind me, as

if Camellia would charge up the stairs and into my room, ready for an altercation.

Maybe she would. I didn't know. To my mind, no one did.

The kind of trauma Camellia had endured could manifest in many different ways. Maybe it already had.

Catherine confided in me that she'd been attacked on the moors. Nurse Gray and Charles insisted it was a fall, but what if it hadn't been?

I'd been dismissive of Catherine's claims from the start just like everyone else, but now I knew there was more going on inside my sister's home than I had realized. There were dark forces at play, and whether they were the spiritual kind touted by the Wilds next door or something of a more human nature, I didn't know. But I would soon find out.

9

Catherine slept through the morning and felt nauseous over lunch. By early afternoon, I'd convinced Nurse Gray to let Catherine go for a walk, but then it began to rain. And rain. And rain.

It was a good soaking rain that puddled on the ground and lashed against the windows. It filled the house with a consistent drumming noise that made everyone feel lazy. Even me. I was not usually one to nap, but when Catherine fell back asleep, I went to my room, locked the door, and slept for a restless hour.

I dreamt I was in my sister's house, in the guest room, taking a nap. Then, the doorknob began to rattle.

In the dream, I sat up in bed, staring at the door, certain Camellia would charge through it at any second, ready to take me to task for talking about her with Charles.

The doorknob would go still for long seconds that stretched to minutes, and I would swear the light outside the window was changing from afternoon to evening to night. Yet, I sat and stared at the knob. When it began turning again, I jumped and let out a shriek.

This happened again and again, until I grew hungry and tired and even bored. I wanted whatever was on the other side of the door to come in already. So, eventually, I gathered my courage and my dressing gown and walked towards the door.

If this is the way I die, I thought, *then let it be the way I die.*

Then, I thrust open the door.

I'd prepared myself for Camellia to be standing outside, but there was nothing. No one at all.

I walked down the hallway, checking the doors as I went, but they were all locked. The usual sounds of shuffling feet or soft voices had been replaced with perfect silence. The kind of silence that felt like a physical presence lurking over one.

After checking the second floor and the main floor, I finally walked outside. The ground was muddy and damp from the rain, but my feet didn't sink into it. I seemed to float above the ground, in fact, my bare feet immune to the cold slime of the mud. I called out for my sister or Charles. At one point, I became so desperate to find another human that I called for my infant niece, as well. No one answered.

The longer I walked, the less I remembered why I was walking at all. I couldn't remember what had sent me out of the house, so I tried to turn around, but the house was gone. In its stead was a smoking pile of rubble with a small pile of bricks in the center that had once been the living room fireplace.

Just as I opened my mouth to scream, something cracked over the back of my head.

At once, whatever dream magic had kept me from sinking into the mud faltered, and I fell flat against the earth. The cold seeped into me, drawing me to sleep, and I listened. I closed my eyes and sunk into the ground as footsteps squelched in the mud around me.

WHEN I WOKE UP, I was shivering.

The fire in my hearth had waned to small embers, and the cool wind that had blown away the rain clouds, also blew open my window. The draft was icy, and I darted across the wood floor in bare feet, slammed the window shut, and then threw myself back beneath the covers to get warm.

I couldn't hear any movement in the rest of the house, and that more than anything propelled me out of bed. I wanted to be sure my dream hadn't come true.

The second I opened the door, I could hear Camellia's singing voice, lulling Hazel back to sleep. I could also hear the confident click of Nurse Gray's heeled shoes on the floor. Charles, I couldn't hear, but I had every reason to believe he was down in his study as usual.

Confident the rest of the house hadn't disappeared, I went back into my room, laced my walking boots on over my stockings, and slipped into my wool coat.

No one stopped me as I tromped through the house and through the back door. I didn't expect they would. Catherine as the only exception, everyone seemed to want me to leave sooner rather than later.

I would not give them what they wanted, but I did require frequent outings to help keep my sanity. Part of me felt Catherine had begun to lose her wits because the house itself was so gloomy.

No one smiled or laughed or joked. It was nothing but glum people coexisting alongside one another without ever really interacting. Nothing like the home I knew Catherine wanted.

If there was any doubt that my dream had been nothing more than a dream, my first step out of the back door was proof enough. Almost immediately, my boots sunk two inches deep in mud.

The ground suctioned around my shoes, pulling at my feet in turn as I moved down the path, but I did not turn back.

I needed a break from the four walls of my room, and I could not spend another second next to my sister's bedside or reading books in the sitting room downstairs, or trying to talk sense into my brother-in-law.

If I was to remain at Catherine's home—a previously and mistakenly described 'picturesque countryside escape'—I needed fresh air and time to think. I needed to remind myself of what was real and what was not.

Despite what Charles said, I knew my sister was not insane.

Camellia's relationship with Hazel was not normal or healthy.

Nurse Gray over-medicated Catherine.

Margaret and Abigail Wilds might be the most normal people I had met during my time in the moors.

Aside from the strange moment we'd shared the last time I'd visited when the women refused to acknowledge the striking similarities between their sister and mine, they had been nothing but open and honest with me. That seemed much more normal than hiding away in dark rooms and not talking to anyone. It seemed a better option than avoiding difficult problems and hoping they went away on their own.

When I reached the fork in the trail, I turned back to the house to be sure it still stood.

The house nearly disappeared in the ominous gray sky. The walls looked pale and lifeless, and each of the windows was like a dark tunnel one could get lost in.

It was not a comforting image, but there were no flames and it remained standing, which gave me some measure of comfort.

When I turned back around, I looked for the carved rock Catherine had said marked the safest trails and followed it through an overhang of trees.

The ground was less wet where the trees had provided some protection from the rain, so my muscles got a small break from slogging through thick, sticky mud. Though, I still had to push aside plenty of branches and climb a number of large rocks. If this was the easier of the two trails, I did not want to know what the other would be like.

My sense of direction had always been woefully poor, so I would trust whichever path Charles had marked without hesitation.

Just as I came out on the other side of the stand of trees, I decided to stop for a rest. The sun had broken through the clouds enough for my skin to feel warm while basking in the light, and I wanted to catch my breath. There was a large rock with a downed tree resting across it, and I perched on the spongy bark like a bench. The back of my skirt was probably getting soiled, but there wasn't anyone to impress all the way out here in the country. It was nothing like the city where anyone could see one at any moment. My appearance mattered less here than it ever had, and that was one good thing about my visit if nothing else.

I wished I'd brought some water with me. Looking at the gathered puddles all over the ground made me wish I could sip from them directly, but I knew better. I'd tried that exact thing as a child, taking large mouthfuls of standing water, and I was ill for over a week. Besides, if I did become ill here, Nurse Gray would likely oversee my recovery, and that was the last thing in the world I wanted.

I never asked Charles how many nurses he'd seen before settling on Nurse Gray, but perhaps I should have. Margaret and Abigail Wilds had given her a recommendation, but they were not exactly women in tune with modern science. What did they know about nursing and health? Very little. Besides, their sister died under Nurse Gray's care.

The thought felt cruel, and I pushed it aside. Nurse Gray could not be blamed for one patient's poor health. It was written into the description of nursing that lives would be lost no matter the quality of the care.

By all accounts, she seemed to care deeply for Catherine. Though, my issue was with how deeply she cared. Too deeply, if anyone asked me. Though, they never did.

I dug the toe of my boot into the soft earth, pushing a large dollop of mud aside, unearthing a long brown worm. I bent to examine it closer, feeling more like a child than I had in years, and I noticed something white in the mud next to it. Using the toe of my boot once again, I sifted small layers of mud away until the object became more discernible.

It was a bone.

A jawbone by the looks of it, though it was small enough with a long curved tooth arcing upward that I knew it belonged to a small animal who had likely met its fate from a predator or a fall from the tall trees above.

I remembered what the Wilds had said about collecting bones on the moor. It seemed a strange way to spend time, but I liked the women and wanted to show them I respected their pastime even if I didn't understand it. So, I plucked the bone from the mud and banged it lightly against the tree trunk to shake off some of the remaining filth. Then, I dropped it into my pocket.

When I started out on my walk again, rather than looking up, I kept my eyes on the ground. It wasn't long before I'd found several other small bones without any digging at all. It seemed the heavy rains had softened the ground and unearthed things. I wasn't skilled enough to know if the bones came from the same animal or from multiple creatures, but I dropped them all in my pocket hoping the sisters would be able to tell me later.

If nothing else, delivering the bones would be another excuse to drop in on Margaret and Abigail. I wanted to ask them more about their experience with Nurse Gray and see if they noticed anything disturbing about her care for Dorothea, and I also wanted to ask them about Dorothea.

It was likely they had no explanation for the physical similarities between their sister and mine, but it seemed too striking not to comment on. Perhaps we shared a distant family lineage. It was rather unlikely that the sisters would have a family genealogy on hand, but it was worth asking.

When my neck began to hurt from looking down at the ground so intently, hunting for bones, I rolled it back and then looked forward. Suddenly, I realized the late afternoon had quickly given way to evening.

I'd been so focused on the ground that I hadn't paid the sky any notice. The sun was dropping below the horizon, painting the sky in deep shades of orange and purple. If I wanted to get back to the house without turning an ankle on the uneven ground, I needed to go now.

As I turned to go, however, a strange cloud to my left caught my attention.

It hung low to the ground and looked to be much closer than the rest of the sky. I puzzled over it for a moment before understanding the deep gray cloud was not a cloud at all, but smoke.

The fading memory of my dream twisted my stomach. Even though I did not believe in the future predicting power of dreams, I couldn't help but feel like I'd expected to see this smoke. And more than that, like I should discover what was causing it.

There was no danger of the fire spreading and overtaking the house. The ground was wet enough from the recent rain that the fire didn't stand a chance of spreading, which begged the question of how it had started in the first place.

I looked back and could see the very top of my sister's house through the trees. It was further away than I would have liked, and I didn't have much time before full dark set in. Yet, I couldn't bring myself to turn and walk back the way I'd come.

With a deep sense of urgency, I turned back around and walked straight for the smoke.

The ground was uneven, rising and falling hills that made it difficult to see too far ahead. Every time I crested a hill, I felt certain the source of the smoke would be revealed, but it was always just behind the next crest. And the next.

As I climbed up them, my legs burning with the effort, my lungs straining in my chest, a distant ringing began in my ears.

With every step, it grew louder and louder. Until I could tell it wasn't a ringing at all. But chanting.

A consistent humming noise not unlike a heartbeat.

Hum-drum. Hum-drum. Hum-drum.

The hair on my arms raised beneath my coat, and I fought off a sudden chill, forcing myself to keep moving even when my instincts screamed for me to retreat.

Finally, after several hills, I struggled up the last one, my boots slipping in the mud so that I had to catch myself on my hands. I climbed to the top and immediately froze.

I froze outwardly and inwardly.

My body did not move, and I was cold through my entire core.

I could see a fire burning in the center of a circle of trees, and around it, a shadow danced.

Or shadows.

Through the small glimpses through tree trunks, I couldn't tell how many there were or...*what* they were.

Black dripped from them, pooling on the ground at their feet.

Catherine spoke of robes when she told me of her attack. She recalled seeing flashes of robes and movement before she was struck on the head.

Was this what she saw?

I crouched down on the hilltop and narrowed my eyes, trying to better make out the shapes to see if they were spectral or human, but I'd lost even more light during my trek to get here, and it was too dark to see much. The fire in the center of the grove illuminated the surroundings, but consequently, cast everything into silhouette.

If Catherine had truly been attacked—had truly encountered something strange or otherworldly—I owed it to her to find out what it was. Right now, she was locked away in her room under the constant care of a nurse because her husband believed her to be ill, but what if that wasn't true? What if her story had been accurate from the start and everyone had simply chosen not to believe it, myself included?

Guilt rippled through me, and the sensation was powerful enough to override my sense of self-preservation. I took a deep breath and began descending the other side of the hill.

I'd taken no more than three steps, however, when a flash of movement at the base of the hill caught my eye.

My heart leapt in my chest, momentarily stealing my breath, and I stopped to examine what it was.

Aside from the distant chanting, all was quiet. Until a violent shrieking tore through the evening air.

The sound was accompanied by hurried movement

only thirty paces away from me. It was a robed figure—
the same one from the fire or another one, I couldn't say
—and it drew nearer to me and then away, repeating the
movement several times, growing closer with each pass.

Horror gripped my soul and consciousness, and I
turned and ran as hard and fast as I could in the opposite
direction.

My curiosity had fled from me the moment the being
had begun to scream, and now all I cared about was
getting back to my sister's house in one piece.

The ground was wet and pocked with footfalls that
sent me sprawling face first into the mud again and again.
Yet, every time, I dragged myself to my feet and continued
my retreat.

I didn't turn to see if the figure was pursuing me, I
simply ran as though it was.

I ran back over the hills, through the trees, and up the
path that led to the back door of the house, and I didn't
realize I'd been screaming until the back door opened.

Light shone out around the figure standing there, and
I didn't care who it was so long as they weren't wearing a
robe. I hurtled up the stairs and threw myself, mud and
all, into the arms of the stranger.

Distantly, I heard Camellia Cresswell shout back into
the house for her brother, but I couldn't remember much
else. Overcome with exhaustion and fear, I closed my
eyes and slipped into darkness.

10

There was smoke. So much smoke I couldn't see or think or breathe.

I blinked against the burning in my eyes and could make out human-like shapes moving around me, but I couldn't see their faces.

I called out for them again and again, begging them to identify themselves, but they refused to say anything beyond their constant chant: *hum-drum, hum-drum.*

When I opened my mouth to scream again, something cool poured through my lips. It was bitter tasting, and I wasn't sure where it came from. If it had anything to do with the shadows dancing around me, I didn't want it, no matter how good it felt in my dry mouth. So, I spit it out.

She won't keep anything down. I've been trying for half an hour.

The voice was familiar. Faint but familiar.

Try again, another voice said. *The last thing Catherine needs is for her sister to take ill, as well.*

Charles. I knew that voice was Charles, and once that information came to me, I could remember the first voice belonged to Nurse Gray.

I strained to open my eyes, trying to wake up, and I heard the voice remark on my movement. It encouraged me to try harder, to press beyond the exhaustion that weighed me down. I needed to tell them what I'd seen, what had happened.

When my eyelids finally fluttered open, I saw Nurse Gray and Charles standing near my bedside. The nurse was standing the closest, with Charles just behind her. When I opened my eyes, he didn't move or rush to my bedside, but looked to the nurse.

"Miss Beckingham?" Nurse Gray asked, lightly touching my shoulder. "You are safe and well. Do not panic."

Those words were rarely uttered to people with no reason to panic, so they did little to comfort me.

"You are in your room," she continued. "Charles and Camellia are here. You're safe."

I blinked several more times, my vision clearing, and then tried to sit myself up in bed. Immediately, my joints protested, and I groaned.

"You fell," Nurse Gray said, not sounding entirely certain. "You have a lot of scrapes and bruises, but no breaks as far as I can see. It would be best for you to stay still and rest. I have this medicine here that should help you—"

"No." My voice was dry and hoarse, but sharp. I shook my head even though the effort made my brain crash against my skull. "No, I'm fine."

"Hardly," Camellia said, finally stepping into view.

Her brow was creased with concern, but she looked almost annoyed with me. "I'm covered in enough blood and mud to prove it. You are not fine at all."

The memory of crashing into the arms of the person standing in the doorway came back to me, and I remembered Camellia's voice. She must have been the person unlucky enough to catch me fresh from my sprint across the moors. I looked down and saw the dried mud on her dress, and despite everything I'd just endured, the sight of it nearly made me laugh.

That feeling, if nothing else, brought me back to myself. It cleared my head and helped me remember what was important.

The truth.

"I saw something. I saw—"

"Shadows," Charles finished.

I turned to him and frowned. "How did you—"

"You were talking in your sleep," Nurse Gray said. "Ramblings and nonsense. You didn't know what you were saying."

She spoke authoritatively, as if she knew what was in my head better than I did. I didn't appreciate it.

Ignoring her earlier warning, I used my weak, bruised arms to lift myself to sitting. My muscles agonized over the movement, and I didn't want to think about how much worse I'd feel in the morning.

"Well, I know what I am saying now, and I saw shadows. On the moors."

Camellia rolled her eyes and crossed her arms, not bothering to hide her disbelief. Charles, however, looked stricken. His eyes were wide and sad, turned down at the corners, and his hands twisted in uncertainty in front of him.

"You were screaming when Camellia found you," he said. "You barely made it into the house before you collapsed. I'm not sure now is the time to talk about what you think you saw."

"What I know I saw," I corrected him. "I was delirious when I made it to the house because I'd run so far. I was exhausted. But I remember very clearly the reason I ran."

Camellia leaned in to her brother, but did not bother to lower her voice or whisper. "This is exactly what happened with Catherine. Perhaps, whatever affliction this is, runs in the family."

Anger reddened my cheeks, and I turned on Camellia, my eyes narrowed. "What affliction would that be, Camellia? Because as far as I'm aware, no one has quite cured whatever it is my sister has come down with. Could that be because there is nothing to cure?"

Charles extended a hand to calm me. "No one meant anything hurtful, Alice. We are just trying to make sense of this."

"Then let me help you." I slammed my fists into the mattress and met each of the three nervous sets of eyes in the room. "Listen to me. Hear my story. When I'm done, you can decide whatever you want, but I won't allow you to discuss what could be happening without listening to what I experienced first."

Once again, Camellia looked bored and annoyed, but Charles nodded. "That is fair, Alice. What did you see?"

"I took a nap this afternoon, and when I woke up, I needed some fresh air. So, I went for a walk before dinner. I followed the trail that you, Charles, marked as being safe, but it was more difficult than I anticipated."

"Could we please move on to the part that made you run screaming into the house?" Camellia asked impatiently.

"Camellia," Charles warned her.

She shrugged. "I'm sorry, but we don't need her to recount her entire day. Just the part that is necessary for the story."

I ignored her to the best of my ability and carried on, telling them about the smoke and the chanting. I told them about the dark figures I saw through the trees.

"This sounds like a children's frightening story," Camellia said, clearly exasperated. She turned to me, hands pressed together. "I'm sure you think you saw these things, Alice, but can't you hear how insane it sounds?"

Suddenly, I understood my sister's broken spirit perfectly.

Since arriving in Yorkshire, I couldn't fathom why my sister, who had never failed to speak her mind or have her voice be heard, was shrinking into a shell. Why she didn't defend herself or argue with her nurse. Why she didn't demand that her husband hear her and act accordingly.

Now, however, it made sense.

Because they—her husband, sister-in-law, and Nurse Gray—had broken her down. They'd made her feel small and silly. Whether they'd meant to or not, they made Catherine feel mad, so she gave up trying.

"Strange and unexpected things happen all the time," I said, eyes focused on Camellia. She, more than anyone, should understand that point. She'd left her home one afternoon for a walk and come back to find it in ruins, her family destroyed. Why, then, did she have such a hard time believing something strange could be happening on the moors?

I'd admit, believing in house fires did not immediately predispose one to believing in spirits, but still, I felt Camellia should have been slightly more on my side given her past trauma.

Charles was still wringing his hands, and despite me saying I did not want any medication, I could see Nurse Gray eyeing the vials on the table.

I sighed. "I know this is a strange story. If it was not strange, I wouldn't have run from the moors screaming as I did. I wouldn't have collapsed from fear and exhaustion."

"You speak in a rational tone, but your words do not make sense to me," Charles admitted, his shoulders stooping forward. "From the window here, we can't see any smoke on the horizon. And the ground is so wet from the rain that I'm not sure any fire could have caught."

It was obvious to me that I was not going to change any minds, so I decided to save my strength. I lowered my head and nodded in solemn agreement, admitting that my time spent with the Wilds may have sparked my imagination.

"It was a long walk from the house to where I was, and I didn't pack any water."

"Thirst has done much worse things to people," Charles said readily, happy to agree with any explanation other than the truth. "That is probably what it was."

"Yes, most likely," I lied. "I just need a glass of water and some rest."

Nurse Gray rushed away to get me water, and I didn't consider until halfway through the glass whether she'd put something in it.

Whether it was from an unknown medication or my physical exhaustion, I didn't know, but I fell into a deep and untroubled sleep.

~

I DIDN'T WAKE until late the next morning.

Warm, golden light poured through the windows, and I could hear birds chirping in the nearby trees.

It sounded like a lovely day, and I was eager to get out of bed.

The second I lifted my arms to stretch, however, my entire body protested. My legs burned with even the slightest movement, and scratches on my arms stung as the skin pulled.

Suddenly, the evening's events rushed back to me in a flurry, and the day didn't seem quite so welcoming. In fact, it felt as though the earth were mocking me. The weather of the previous day—lashing rain and gray skies —would have been much more suited for how I felt.

Slowly, I peeled back my blankets and assessed myself.

Nurse Gray must have changed my clothes and tended to my wounds before I'd awoken from my bout of unconsciousness because, where I should have been caked in earth and blood, there was nothing but pink skin marred with cuts and deep bruises. I slid my hands over the small welts, wincing when I pressed on some of the more painful bruises.

I slid my legs to the side and lowered my feet to the floor, moving slowly to let my body grow accustomed to movement once again. Not only had the previous day's exercise been more than I was used to, but the repeated falling during my clumsy escape had taken a toll on me. I would need to move slowly to avoid hurting myself further.

Long minutes passed as I rolled my ankles, flexed my calves, and stretched out my thighs. My arms received the same treatment, and by the time twenty minutes had gone by, I felt much more capable. I still smarted when I turned too quickly or squatted down to pull stockings from the bottom drawer, but it was not unbearable.

I dressed in a simple cotton dress that did not require any buttoning or tucking or fussing. It simply needed to be pulled over my head, which made my shoulders ache, and then it was done. Fastening my shoes required a good deal of movement I wasn't prepared for, though. I rested on the side of my bed and drew my knee up to my chest to tie the laces of my two-toned oxfords, and even then, I had to take several breaks to let my leg relax.

When I was finally dressed, I pinned back the wild mess of curls on my head and went down to breakfast.

I didn't look as polished as I would have liked, but no one would expect much else from me today. Not after everything I'd been through the day before.

Breakfast was likely already over, but I hoped there would be some bread and fruit remaining, at least. My stomach rumbled with hunger, and more than any medication or rest, I needed sustenance to heal.

I didn't make any effort to walk especially quietly, but I had to take such slow steps to make sure I didn't go light headed and lose my balance, that Camellia and Charles must not have heard my approach. For when I reached the top of the stairs, their hushed voices carried up to me.

"I think we are worrying about something we ought not to worry about yet," Charles said.

"And I think you are once again avoiding a situation you find uncomfortable for no other reason than that you'd rather not deal with it," came the response.

"Don't forget whose house this is, Camellia," Charles warned.

"Nurse Gray agrees with me," Camellia went on. "We spoke last night, and she thinks we should keep a close eye on Alice. She hasn't seemed well since she arrived."

Since I arrived? My face wrinkled in displeasure. Who was Camellia to decide whether I was well or not? She didn't even know me.

"That is just Alice's way," Charles said, coming to my defense, though it didn't feel quite like a defense. It still felt like an insult. "She is an odd girl, outspoken and commanding. But I've never seen her like I did last night. Something happened to her."

"Madness," Camellia whispered harshly. "That apparently runs in the family."

Charles sighed loudly.

"It is no fault of yours, brother. You could not have known you were marrying into a family with these kinds of emotional and mental troubles. You shouldn't blame yourself."

At that, I was about to charge down the stairs and tell Camellia exactly what I thought of her. If she wanted to say my family had problems, what of hers?

She'd lost her family in a fire and was clearly trying to

replace them with another family rather than face her own grief. If she wanted to discuss emotional and mental troubles, then I was more than happy to accommodate her.

However, just before I could stomp down the stairs, alerting the couple to my presence, Camellia continued speaking. "As I said, Nurse Gray is in agreement. We should keep both women away from Hazel until we can figure out how to help them."

"Catherine would never hurt our daughter," Charles said passionately.

"Catherine wouldn't," Camellia agreed. "But the woman in that room is not the same Catherine anymore. She has changed. You and I have both seen it since my arrival. Even since Alice's arrival, she has changed."

"She does seem to be wilting away."

"Especially over the last week." It was not difficult to understand what Camellia was implying. She thought I, for whatever reason, was causing my sister to decline even further.

"I don't want to tell you how to manage your own home, but I think it would be wise to keep Alice away from your wife and, especially, your child until we know she is safe."

"Alice wouldn't hurt anyone," Charles said, though his voice was weak. It sounded as though he barely believed what he was saying. "I don't believe that is necessary."

"Perhaps not, but isn't it better to be cautious now rather than sorry later?"

I wanted to go down and argue on my own behalf, but I knew it wouldn't do any good. Besides, I wanted to speak to Catherine, and if Camellia got her way, soon enough, I wouldn't be allowed to.

I tiptoed across the hallway to my sister's room and pushed open the door, but the second I tried to step inside, I was accosted by Nurse Gray.

The petite woman was surprisingly formidable, and she forced me into the hallway without ever physically touching me. She walked forward with long steps, making me walk backwards so we didn't run into one another. Once I was in the middle of the hallway, she pulled Catherine's door shut behind her.

"I was just coming to check on you," she said. "I'm glad to see you had a good night's rest."

I studied her face for any sign of whether or not she'd slipped some of her sleep aid into my water, but her face was blank and clinical.

"I had an unnaturally deep sleep," I said. "I slept through breakfast, which I've never done before."

"To be expected," Nurse Gray said matter-of-factly. "You endured a great deal yesterday, and your body needs time to recover. In fact, you should go back to bed now. I'll have breakfast brought to your room."

She held out her hand, ready to lead me back to my room, but I dodged her. "Actually, I feel well enough to go downstairs."

She clicked her tongue at me. "The worst thing anyone can do for recovery is to overexert oneself too soon. Believe me, I've seen it done time and time again. No, it will be better for you to rest today."

As much as I wanted to remind Nurse Gray that she was not hired to be my nurse and that perhaps she should mind her own business, I felt quarreling with the woman would be an even bigger overexertion than going down to breakfast. She would not give up without a fight, and even if I did win, my prize would be spending time with Charles and Camellia minutes after they'd been "secretly" discussing my sanity.

I wasn't sure I felt comfortable with that experience yet. They would probably take my awkwardness as yet another sign that I was mentally unfit to go near my own sister. For right now, as much as I didn't want to agree with Nurse Gray, the best thing for me to do would be to remain in my room for awhile longer.

Sensing my resignation, Nurse Gray pressed her cold hand to the middle of my back and directed me back to my room.

11

Nurse Gray delivered tea with my breakfast, and despite the thirst burning in the back of my throat, I didn't drink it. I had things to do and could not waste the day in sleep. So, when she left me to eat, I poured the tea from my bedroom window.

The toast, however, I ate readily. I slathered it in warm butter and jam and couldn't believe how much more like myself I felt once I was done. My muscles still ached and the bruises and scratches I'd earned from my run through the moors still stung when I allowed my mind to focus on them, but on the whole, I felt recovered enough. I wouldn't dare say such a thing to Nurse Gray, though.

When she came back for my breakfast tray, I feigned sleep. I threw one arm over my eyes and pressed my cheek into my pillow, facing away from the door. She hesitated next to my bed, watching my breathing. I must have convinced her because, a moment later, she took my tray and left the room. Then, knowing she would not check on me for a while, I listened at the door for her footsteps to descend the stairs. Once they did, I slipped out of my room and crossed the hall to Catherine's.

The curtains were drawn when I walked in, the room dark, but I saw movement in front of one of the windows. The figure turned, wide eyes glowing in the darkness, and I realized it was Catherine. When she saw it was me, her expression smoothed over and she turned back to the curtains and pulled them open all at once.

Light streamed in, blinding me, and I squinted against it.

"I thought you were Nurse Gray."

"She went downstairs," I said.

Catherine nodded and turned back to me. "I know. I've been pretending to drink my mid-morning cup of tea and waiting for her to leave so I can walk about the room. If it were up to her, I think I'd sleep my life away."

"I wasn't sure it was necessary, but I skipped my own tea so I could come and see you," I admitted. "She does dose it with something, then?"

"She must," Catherine said. "I'm ready every morning to begin my day, but after that tea, all I want to do is lie back down. I'm sure she means well, but I'm tired of being tired."

I wasn't so sure Nurse Gray did mean well, but I also had more important things to discuss with Catherine. Luckily, she broached the subject herself.

"What happened to you?" she asked, eyes narrowed at my appearance. She walked forward slowly, careful not to stamp on the wood floor and alert anyone downstairs to movement, and touched her hand to my cheek. "You are covered in scratches. I heard some commotion last night, but Nurse Gray told me it was nothing to worry about."

I motioned for Catherine to sit down in the rocking chair in the corner, the one usually reserved for Nurse Gray, while I perched on the edge of her bed.

"You're being cryptic," she said nervously. "Are you all right?"

"Beyond some bruises and scratches, yes. I'm fine and so is everyone else."

Catherine took a shallow breath and nodded, relieved.

"However, something has happened, and I want to hear your opinion on the matter."

"Everyone else already knows?" It was more a statement than a question, and her mouth pinched into a tight line at being left out of household discussions.

"I wanted to come to you immediately, but they were worried it might upset you."

"Alice, please. Out with it. I don't want to live in this suspense forever. If everyone else already knows, I don't want to be in the dark for another—"

"I saw something out on the moors."

My sister's mouth hung open, words still unspoken, but her eyes were expressive enough on their own. They widened until I could see a ring of white around the blue, alert and focused on my face. "What did you see?"

"I'm not sure," I said honestly. "I ran away before I could understand what it was exactly, hence the scratches and bruises. The commotion you heard last night was me being brought in by Camellia and Charles. I don't remember much of it until I woke up in bed later with Nurse Gray by my bedside. They think I'm mad, Cat."

She flinched at the word and then nodded for me to continue.

"I saw figures dancing around a fire, dark robes, and I heard...screaming. Screeching, really. It chilled me to my bones, and I couldn't stay to investigate. I ran." I gripped my knee and shook my head. "I'm sorry. I wanted to stay to solve this all for you, but I couldn't."

"I'm glad you didn't," Catherine said, standing up and pacing across the room.

"You are?"

She nodded and lowered her head, eyes cast to the floor. "My mind was muddled for so long because of exhaustion and the medications and fear, but as I've stopped taking so many of Nurse Gray's draughts, my thoughts have cleared, and I'm no longer certain of what I saw."

Catherine spoke nervously, her words disjointed in strange places, as though she was forcing the words out. As though she was trying to recall some half-memorized speech.

"What do you mean?"

"I mean..." her shoulders drooped, and she sighed wearily, the sound coming from her very core. "I mean that I am no longer certain of what happened to me. Not as certain as I am that my story as it was upset everyone in my life. If I carry on speaking of ghosts, my family will fall apart. I will waste away in this room, memorizing the patterns of the wallpaper."

"Catherine."

"No." My sister held up her hand to quiet me. "I've made up my mind. Exhaustion overtook me on my walk, and I fell and hit my head on a rock. Just as everyone said. I have no proof anything else happened, so—"

"I am your proof!" I said a bit too loudly. Catherine flinched and glanced towards the door, reminding me why she was saying any of this in the first place. Because my sister was afraid to exist in her own home. I pressed a hand to my chest and softened my voice, speaking earnestly. "I saw something yesterday that I can't explain, Catherine. I saw things that mimicked the story you told, and I believe you. I know I didn't at the start, but I am telling you now that I do."

Catherine stared at me for a long moment, her blue eyes pale and sad. Then, she crossed the room and took my hands in hers. She studied our entangled fingers for awhile before she ran her thumbs over my knuckles and looked up at me. "You believe me, and now *they* think you're mad, too."

She dropped my hands and walked back to the rocking chair, lowering herself slowly like she was a much older woman. "My guess is that Nurse Gray is downstairs right now working on a theory of shared delusion. She and Charles and Camellia would sooner believe that than believe in ghosts. They are not like the Wilds."

The casual mention of her neighbors caught me by surprise. According to the Wilds sisters, Catherine had not been to see them for a very long time, although Charles still made regular visits. How much did she know about their beliefs?

"Have you spoken to Margaret and Abigail about what you saw?"

Catherine shook her head. "There was no need. I knew they would believe me. The first time I met them they became convinced I was the reincarnation of their dead sister."

"Dorothea?" The likeness between Dorothea Wilds and Catherine had been uncanny to me, but the women had treated it as insignificant. Now, it was clear they believed differently. Or, at least, used to believe differently.

Catherine shrugged and waved a hand. "I'm not sure. They made me uncomfortable with such talk, so I stopped visiting them. The point is, Alice, that no one here in this household believes in such things, and I'm not so sure I do, either."

"You truly believe you fell and hit your head on a rock, then?"

Her mouth opened, ready with an answer, and then closed. Finally, she spoke on a sigh. "Maybe it was a rock or maybe I was attacked. I don't know anymore, but it doesn't matter."

"How can it not matter if you were attacked?"

"Because I'm safe now," she said. "As soon as I prove to them all that I am not insane—that I've come to my senses—life will continue on as it was before."

"You said the house was cursed, Cat. You told me when I arrived that you needed me, and now—"

"Now," Catherine said, interrupting me. "It may be time for you to go back to London."

Seeing shadows and figures on the moor had not made me feel insane, but suddenly, I felt absolutely mad.

I'd come into my sister's home to correct a problem that no one else seemed to think was a problem anymore. Even my own sister who was willing to admit she may have been attacked by an unknown person, didn't seem to concern herself with finding out who it was or for what reason they may have wanted to attack her.

"I'm sorry I sent you that message and asked you to come here. This was never your problem to solve, and I shouldn't have sent for you."

"You should have sent for me sooner," I corrected. "Long before things got to this state. You may be fine with the way things are going in this house, but I'm not. Because I was there all those years when you grew up daydreaming about your future, and never once did it involve a shabby house in the country with no friends and a personal nurse."

"Alice." Catherine's words were a warning, but I couldn't stop. If I did, I was afraid I'd never get to say what was on my mind. What needed to be said.

"I know Charles is a good man, but he is allowing his sister and your nurse to run this house. He is allowing your voice to be drowned out, and I can't leave you here like this knowing you aren't happy."

"How do you know I'm not happy?" Catherine's face was flushed, and I didn't know if it was with anger or fever. What if she really was ill and my angering her was making it worse?

"Because you are locked away in this room, not even allowed to be a mother to your own child."

Her cheeks burned scarlet, and now I knew for certain it was rage on her face. Frustration and embarrassment.

"Get out, Alice."

I shook my head.

"Get out," she repeated. "I've been understanding up

until this point, but now I am ready for you to leave. You are making things more difficult for me."

"I am the only person who is willing to tell you the truth."

Her lip curled back in anger, an expression I'd seen time and time again in my youth, usually after I'd snuck into her room and taken one of her dolls or rearranged her jewelry. Though, I hadn't seen this look in years.

I knew my sister better than almost anyone, and I knew she wasn't happy with the way things were going. More than that, I knew she didn't really believe her "accident" on the moors was no longer a mystery worth solving. Catherine simply wanted to make everyone else comfortable, something the Catherine I knew never would have bothered herself with. I suspected it came from her desire to be part of the family again. To be part of the life happening inside of her house, including her daughter's.

Catherine would do anything to be with her husband and child again, including ignoring her own thoughts and fears in favor of assuaging theirs.

I, however, didn't have the same impulse. My loyalty would always and forever be to my sister, whether she wanted it or not.

Rather than continuing to argue, Catherine stamped loudly on the floor several times. It took me a second to realize what she was doing, but then I heard the footsteps on the stairs. Nurse Gray was coming.

❧

"I THINK my visits with Abigail and Margaret Wilds

stirred my imagination. Their tales of spirits on the moors came to the forefront of my mind as soon as it became dark and I realized I was lost."

Camellia looked at her brother, eyebrows drawn together in suspicion, but Charles' face was flooded with obvious relief. He smiled and nodded, encouraging me to continue.

"Then, when I spoke with Catherine and realized she no longer believed she'd been attacked, I began to see how silly I was being."

Catherine leaned into Charles' side, and he laid a hand on his wife's knee, squeezing it tenderly.

It felt like a betrayal to be sitting in front of all of them and lying. To convince them that they'd been right all along—that Catherine had been unwell and in need of medical intervention in order to find clarity. However, there was no other way. If I wanted to have any kind of freedom within the walls of this house again, I had to lie now. I had to lure them all into complacency.

The plan came to me the moment Nurse Gray walked into Catherine's room.

Her eyes had been narrowed in displeasure, like she was our mother and had caught us sneaking puddings before dinner. But when I'd told her our revelation, she'd been amazed. As had Catherine.

"What are you doing?" my sister had whispered as we walked down the stairs to the sitting room, the rest of the household gathering at the behest of Nurse Gray, who was eager to show off the success of all of her work.

Catherine didn't have as many worries now that Hazel was in her arms, though. Her daughter was bouncing on her lap, her husband was stroking his finger along her knee, and for the first time in a very long time, there were smiles in the room.

Except for Camellia.

"Is this really true, Catherine?" she asked softly. "You seemed so certain of your story just earlier this week when your sister arrived. What changed your mind?"

"Clearly it was Alice," Charles said, winking at me. "Catherine called for her sister because she knew what she needed more than we did. Alice arrived and helped set things right."

"But just last night—"

Charles cleared his throat and turned on his sister, shaking his head. Everyone knew what had happened last night, but he still didn't want to dampen the happy moment with talk of the past. Which was how I knew no one in this house would ever talk about Catherine's accident again if I didn't do it. They would never think twice about the shadows and the robes and the blow to Catherine's head, because it was easier not to.

Which was exactly why the task had now fallen to me.

"Alice and Nurse Gray both helped me tremendously," Catherine said, tipping her head towards the nurse. "Without her care, I likely wouldn't have survived my accident."

Nurse Gray stepped out of the shadows and smiled, grateful for the recognition, though I could see the reality of her situation dawning. Soon enough, she'd be released from her position and sent to the next house.

"Speaking of my duties, it is time to tend to Miss Beckingham's injuries." The nurse laid a hand on my shoulder and directed me out of my chair and towards the stairs, tipping her head to her employers who were cuddling their baby girl in their laps. Camellia Cresswell was the only one who watched us go, her brow lowered in thought.

Nurse Gray wasn't the only one who would be out of a job soon. Now that Hazel's mother was cured, Camellia would once again be simply an aunt. I wondered how the women would acclimate to their new roles.

12

C atherine's recovery was announced on Saturday, and by Sunday, she was ready to get out of the house.

"I haven't been into town in too long to remember, and I haven't set foot in the little church even longer than that," she said.

"She was so uncomfortable at the end of her pregnancy that we didn't even consider making the drive into the village," Charles explained to me as he handed his wife another scone with a large dollop of cream atop it.

"Now," Catherine continued eagerly, adding a spoonful of jam before taking a large bite. "I want everything to return to the usual."

Charles clapped his hands together, smiling like I hadn't seen him smile since my arrival. "In that case, it seems like today would be a lovely day for us all to attend services together."

Catherine nodded in agreement.

"All of us?" Camellia asked.

For a moment, I thought she was asking whether she would be going with them, but then she turned to me, and I understood. Her eyes flicked from the large scratch I knew was on my forehead to the series of smaller scratches along my chest and neck.

"I don't think I'm feeling up to it today," I said, saving everyone the awkward conversation of whether or not I should attend. Not only did I not want to explain to a group of strangers that I'd scratched up my arms and face while running from ghosts through the moors, but I also wouldn't mind the time alone. With Camellia, Nurse Gray, Charles, and now, even Catherine, constantly watching me and monitoring me as though I was a spy sent to ferret information out of the house rather than a guest invited to come here, having time to myself where I didn't have to constantly fret over what I said and did would be nice.

"Nurse Gray can stay with her," Charles said, laying a hand over Catherine's, easing her concerns before they could even be spoken.

Catherine frowned. "But she hasn't been to a service for just as long as I have. And you know how devout she is."

"I do not need a nurse," I said. "Nurse Gray helped me clean and dress some of the deeper cuts this morning, and they won't need any tending until this evening. I can manage myself."

"Are you sure?" Catherine asked.

"Yes," Camellia agreed. "I don't know if it is wise to leave her here alone."

"*She* will be fine," I said, doing my best not to roll my eyes at Camellia. I had never enjoyed being spoken of in the third person, and I especially didn't like when it was done by Camellia. "I'm a grown woman, remember. I know how to keep myself busy for a few hours. All of you, go into the village and stay as long as you like. I'll find ways to occupy my time."

And once everyone was dressed—Catherine donning a fashionable crepe paper dress that fell in tight ruffles around her shins and a cloche hat with a matching green flower—they loaded into the car and pulled away, leaving me on my own for the first time in a week.

Though, I wasn't entirely alone. As soon as I closed the front door, I heard the sound of a pan banging in the kitchen, and I remembered my sister's small household staff had remained behind, as well. The nanny was upstairs in her room, no doubt taking a nap since Charles and Catherine had taken Hazel with them to church, but the maid and cook would be nearby, probably cleaning up after breakfast.

Even though I'd just been thinking about the benefits of a morning alone, I found myself pushing open the swinging door into the kitchen.

The maid—a young girl with short brown hair tucked close to her face and a white cap obscuring her curls—startled when the door opened, dropping a plate into the sink and sloshing water up onto the countertop.

"I didn't realize anyone was still here," she said, scrambling to pick up the plate before she thought better of it and wiped her hands on a dish towel to dry them. She walked to the end of the counter at once and lowered her head. "Can I help you, Miss Beckingham?"

"No. Please, go on with your work. I didn't mean to interrupt you."

She seemed hesitant, but after a few seconds of silence, she went back to the sink and continued cleaning. Her movements were stiff and uncomfortable, and it seemed strange to me that my sister would run such an ordered home. Catherine had never exactly mingled with our household staff, but she'd never felt the need to be formal. We followed in my mother's lead that way.

"What's your name?" I asked.

Her eyes were wide and gray, and they darted around the room like those of a nervous doe, ready to run off and hide at any second. "Florence."

"Lovely to meet you, Florence."

"You too, Miss Beckingham."

"Alice," I corrected.

She nodded and went back to washing dishes. Her black sleeves were rolled to the elbows, and her pale skin was red from the hot water. I glanced around the room, expecting to see someone else but it appeared she was alone with the small mountain of dirty dishes.

"I thought my sister and brother employed a cook, as well?"

"They do," Florence said. "But she does not come in until lunch. I am not a skilled cook, but breakfast is a simple meal."

"I'd say you are quite skilled. The scones were perfect."

Her face flushed with pleasure and she gave me a quick smile. "I'm glad you enjoyed them, Miss."

The conversation drifted into silence again, and I wasn't entirely sure why I'd come into the kitchen at all. To meet the staff who had been serving me for the last week, certainly, but beyond that, why was I lurking in the doorway and making the poor maid uncomfortable?

"Are you sure there is nothing I can help you with, Miss Beckingham?"

"Alice, please," I said.

Florence's lips pressed together, and she shook her head. "I'm sorry, but the lady of the house really insists on proper addresses. She wouldn't like me speaking to a guest in such a friendly way."

I frowned. "My sister was never so strict before. Besides, if she takes issue with it, I will be sure to tell her that I insisted upon it."

Florence's mouth opened, her dark eyebrows flicking upward, and then she twisted her lips to the side uncomfortably. "I'm sorry. I meant Mr. Cresswell's sister, Camellia."

My frown deepened. "In that case, be sure to call me Alice. I know Camellia lives here now, but you are hired by her brother, correct?"

The maid's eyes were glued to the dish water now, though her hands had gone still beneath the surface. She nodded.

"Then, it seems to me you are to take orders from him and his wife before anyone else."

The maid nodded again, and I could practically see her trembling. I felt badly for giving her such conflicting orders, but the idea that Camellia felt she could command my sister's staff on how to behave bothered me more than it ought.

I stepped towards the sink, head down, and voice low. "I'm sorry, Florence. If I can admit something to you—I'm rather not fond of Camellia. I didn't mean to raise my voice to you."

The maid's eyes went wide with alarm, and she looked up, studying my face as though she couldn't decide whether what I was saying was a trap or not. She must have determined it wasn't because her thin lips turned up into a quick smile.

"That's all right. I'm quite used to raised voices now that a certain person has joined the household."

The statement was quick and flatly told, but it cut straight to the truth, and I had to hold back a wicked laugh.

"Camellia is a woman who...is unafraid to make it known what she wants," I added.

Florence's mouth curled into a genuine grin, and her eyes flared with sarcasm as she nodded in agreement. "Yes, a trait I find to be one of her most admirable."

That time, I really couldn't hold back my laugh. "Truly. She has so many *admirable* qualities it is hard to rank them."

After a week of mostly holding my tongue, it felt good to voice my thoughts, even if they were hidden behind double speak.

I laughed again and added. "As if we were not lucky enough with only Camellia, Nurse Gray has a temperament to match."

I thought the joke had been funny, but the moment I spoke the Nurse's name, Florence's face fell. She rinsed off a dish and set it out on a rack to dry, making no move to join in my teasing.

"I'm sorry, Florence. I was only teasing. Nurse Gray is

a fine woman. She has to be in order to care for people as she does."

If possible, Florence's mouth pressed together even tighter, as though she was holding in words that were desperate to rush out. I wished I could lean forward and unpin her lips to release them.

"Is she a friend of yours?"

"No." Her eyes were wide, as if she were shocked that I could think such a thing. She dried her hands again and shook her head. "I'm sorry, Miss Beck—Alice. I just cannot tease about a woman like Nurse Gray."

"Because it wouldn't be right?" I asked. "Given what she does for a living? I know she saves lives, but—"

"It wouldn't be *safe*," Florence said on a whisper.

A shiver ran down my neck, though I couldn't say exactly why. Nurse Gray had been living with and working for my sister and her family for months and no one had been hurt. Well, Catherine had the accident, but—

An impossibility lodged itself in my mind and refused to be moved.

"Why wouldn't it be safe?"

Florence shook her head and tried to go back to the dishes, but I couldn't let her avoid this question. I walked around the counter so I was standing next to her and grabbed her shoulder, turning her towards me. "If there is something going on here that you know about, I should know, too. If my sister is in danger, then she deserves to know."

"I don't *know* anything," Florence said. "But there are rumors around these parts about Nurse Gray. Stories my mother told me long before that woman came to work for the Cresswells."

"Stories about what?"

Florence blinked, her gray eyes serious. "Death."

"She is a nurse. Death is to be expected."

"Maybe." She shrugged. "But there are a great many nurses who are not known as harbingers of death. They are not whispered about behind their backs the way Nurse Gray is."

Abigail and Margaret had told me Nurse Gray had a lot of spirits around her, and although I still didn't know if I believed in such things, I'd assumed it was because of her line of work, but what if it was something else?

"What do people whisper?"

"Just that," Florence said. "They whisper that she cannot darken a doorstep without someone dying. Her profession is to heal, but she only brings death. When Mrs. Cresswell was found out on the moors, bloody and unconscious, I'd thought it was the curse claiming her. Thank the Heavens she survived, but now there is no way to know which one of us is next."

Florence had been shy when I'd first walked into the kitchen, but I'd clearly broken down the barrier between us. She seemed to have no trouble at all speaking freely now.

"Are there records of Nurse Gray's employment before coming here? Anything to verify how many people have died in her care?"

"I know only what I've heard," Florence said. She leaned in, looking up at me from beneath her lowered brows. "If I were you, I'd head back to London sooner rather than later."

I thanked Florence for her input and excused myself quickly. Mostly because the girl's sudden switch from shy maid to ominous soothsayer made me uncomfortable in more ways than one.

When I'd first come into the house, Catherine had told me she believed the house was cursed and everyone was in danger. Could it be that she'd felt whatever strange phenomenon Florence was discussing? Could such a phenomenon even exist?

Surely, in a profession like nursing, one had to reckon with the fact that some patients were going to be too ill to help. Sometimes—and perhaps even most of the time—people were going to die due to natural causes, and it might just so happen that the nurse was the last one to see them alive.

Could Nurse Gray really be blamed for such a natural occurrence?

I passed by Nurse Gray's temporary guest room on the way to my own and then retraced my steps, stopping in front of it.

I'd never been inside the woman's room. Never even seen inside of it.

Nurse Gray spent the majority of her day in Catherine's room or, occasionally, taking breaks downstairs or in the garden when Catherine needed to rest.

As I reached for the doorknob, I told myself it was nothing more than a curiosity to see the rest of my sister's house that compelled me to open the door. Nothing more than a desire to see where the woman who had tended to my wounds and helped me in my time of need slept.

Except, when I opened the door and stepped inside, I

did not turn on the light. I closed the door silently behind me and pressed my back to it, blending into the shadows.

I'd seen Nurse Gray leave in the car with my sister and the rest of the household, but I still held my breath and studied the bed to make sure there wasn't a human shape lurking beneath it.

The bed was small and modest, and the blanket was tucked crisply beneath the mattress. I'd expected nothing less from Nurse Gray. There was a trunk at the foot of the bed, a small table next to it, and a single lamp. Beneath the table was a black leather bag with two rounded handles clasped together.

It was the medical bag she carried with her into Catherine's room every day. The one I'd seen inside several times. Inside was nothing more than bandages, cleaning supplies, and vials of various medications. Nothing unusual or noteworthy.

I turned instead to the trunk.

It was the only other piece of furniture in the room that belonged to the nurse and hadn't been provided by my sister and brother-in-law. I could tell because the name GRAY was etched into the leather straps that wrapped around it and buckled in the front.

I knelt down in front of the trunk in the dark and undid the straps quietly, lifting the lid and wincing when it banged against the footboard.

It didn't really matter. If Florence heard the noise from downstairs, she'd assume it was me moving upstairs. I didn't need to be perfectly silent and covert since the house was mostly empty. Still, guilt gnawed at my stomach and made even my breathing sound far too loud in my own ears.

Identical gray dresses were folded in a stack in one corner next to matching caps. Stockings were rolled up in another corner along with a second pair of black leather shoes that matched the pair she'd worn to church that morning.

Nurse Gray, it seemed, was as pragmatic in her personal life as in her professional one. She didn't seem to have "work clothes" and "ordinary clothes." Instead, everything was the same drab gray color.

In one sense, she lived with her patients, so it made sense for her to always be in her nursing garb. In another, it seemed like a very small life to lead, never doing anything beyond your occupation.

And Nurse Gray had been in the occupation for a great many years. Long enough that she'd cared for Dorothea Wilds when the three sisters were still young. Or, at least, I assumed that to be the case since the picture of Dorothea they kept on their walls was her as a young woman.

The trunk appeared to be nothing more than clothes, but just as I was about to close the lid, I caught sight of a brown leather folder pressed against the wooden side of the trunk. It was the same color as the wood, so I'd nearly missed it, but now it seemed obvious to me.

I pulled out the folder and unwound the leather cord, feeling more and more guilty by the second for snooping through Nurse Gray's things because of nasty rumors and tales. But that wasn't enough to stop me. The guilt didn't keep me from opening the folder in my lap like it was a book and flipping greedily through the pages.

The pages were soft and yellowed with age and the ink was fading, but I could still make it out.

Each line contained a name, presumably of a patient she'd cared for. Next to it was the date she began working for them and the date her employment ended. At the far right, there was either a single dot or a cross.

Early on in the book, the symbol at the far right was almost always a dot. Then, several pages in, they changed to black crosses. Then, there was nothing but black crosses for pages.

Nurse Gray's time with the patients with the crosses was usually short—just a few months at a time. Sometimes only weeks.

As I scanned the pages, a name caught my eye: Dorothea Wilds.

As I'd suspected, it had been many years since Nurse Gray had cared for Dorothea Wilds. She had the start date of her employment and the end date, and then, at the far right of the page, a cross.

It dawned on me suddenly what the cross meant.

Death.

The dots and crosses kept record of the final outcome of Nurse Gray's patients, and with every page I flipped through, it became clear that the result was overwhelmingly death.

Finally, I reached the end of the ledger, my stomach twisted into knots, and I saw my sister's name. The date read several months earlier and there was a second date written next to it with a dot at the far right, as though Nurse Gray had expected her work to be finished. Then, later, that date and dot were crossed out.

Likely, when Catherine's accident had occurred and Nurse Gray had been asked to continue her work with the family.

I was staring at the crossed out dot, ominous thoughts filling my head, when a creak in the hallway outside caught my attention.

I jolted to alertness and turned to the partially opened window in the room. The sun was much higher in the sky than I'd realized. Had a car rumbled towards the house? I couldn't recall it, but I also couldn't recall hearing anyone come up the stairs?

Panic gripped my heart, but I had the presence of mind to close the folder and replace it in the trunk where it belonged. Then, I closed the trunk, hastily latching it, and spun just as the door opened.

I had no explanation prepared for why I was kneeling at the foot of Nurse Gray's bed. I could tell her I was praying, thanking God for allowing her to heal me, but there was no excuse for why I'd do such a thing in her room.

When Camellia Cresswell walked into the room, twin feelings of relief and dread filled me.

Relief that I didn't have to face Nurse Gray, and dread that the person in the house who, perhaps, wanted me gone most of all, had found me in such a compromising position.

"Alice?" she asked, her voice half-scolding. "What on Earth are you doing in here?"

She had her Bible folded in her hands, pressed against the white lace material of her dress. Her cloche hat shielded her eyes enough that I couldn't exactly make out the expression on her face. Though, considering the circumstances, I could guess that it held surprise and some amount of amusement.

"My bandage came undone, and I was looking for another," I said, the excuse coming to me all at once. "I wasn't sure where Nurse Gray kept them. I tried not to disturb her things."

Camellia lifted a hand and pointed to the black bag under the bed. "Her medical bag is there. In the open."

Her voice was filled with suspicion, and I knew she doubted my story, but I didn't care. I just needed to get out of there.

I stood up, dusting my knees and ignoring the ache in my joints at being curled up on the floor for so long. I hoped Camellia couldn't see the proof of how long I'd been in the room in my stilted movements. "I can't believe I missed that. But now that you are all home, I will just have Nurse Gray do it for me."

"Yes," Camellia said coolly. "That would probably be best. She is outside with the rest of the family. Shall I go tell her to meet you in her room?"

"No, that won't be necessary," I said as evenly as I could manage.

As much as I hated to admit it, I'd been careless, and Camellia had caught me in a low moment. Now, she had every right to march down the stairs and announce to everyone that I'd broken the trust of the household. That I'd done something worthy of being sent back to London immediately. Nothing would bring her greater pleasure, I was sure.

She nodded and stepped aside as I left the room, making sure I went ahead of her, as though she didn't trust me to leave on my own. As soon as I was out in the corridor, she pulled the door closed tightly behind her.

We stood there for a moment, staring at one another, unsure how to proceed. Then, Camellia, lifted her chin, looking me directly in the eyes for the first time. "Perhaps, it would be more appropriate if you stayed in the public rooms of the house from now on."

Then, without another word, she turned on her heel and walked into her own bedroom, closing the door behind her.

13

I stayed in my room for a long time, expecting someone to come and find me.

Either Nurse Gray because she was sent for by Camellia. Or Charles and Catherine because Camellia told them what I'd done.

I expected someone to come, but no one ever did.

When I heard laughter coming from outside, I opened my window but couldn't see who was making the sound. So, I crept from my room to the top of the stairs and could catch a glimpse of my sister and her husband sitting on the front porch with Hazel standing on cloth-covered feet between them. Charles was holding her up, bouncing her until she giggled, and they all looked so happy together.

"You asked to see me, Nurse Gray?"

I recognized the voice of the housemaid, Florence, coming from downstairs, and then Nurse Gray stepped into view. She was standing in the entryway, her hands folded behind her back, her usual gray dress ironed flat and perfect.

I stepped away from the landing so I could only barely see them through the railing, hoping they wouldn't see me.

"I did," the nurse said sternly.

Florence tipped her head, and I couldn't decide if her fear was obvious or if I was only projecting what I'd learned onto her. She seemed to cower in front of the woman. To shrink into herself more than usual.

"I wanted to remind you of our agreement that I would tend to my own room," Nurse Gray said. "You are not to so much as make my bed, do you hear? It is my space."

"I understand, Nurse Gray. Has there been a problem? Is there a reason you are—"

"You know very well the reason," Nurse Gray said with more venom than I'd ever heard from the woman. "My room was not in the order in which I left it, and I do not appreciate you slipping in there the moment I left the house."

"Nurse Gray, I didn't—"

"And you won't do it again," the nurse said, cutting Florence off. "We are finished here."

Nurse Gray stomped into the sitting room, and after a few quiet seconds, I leaned forward to see what had happened to Florence. As soon as I did, my eyes met the maid's through the railing. She was looking up at where I stood, hurt and fear obvious on her face. She'd just confessed to me her fear of the woman, and now I'd made them enemies.

I wanted to rush down and apologize to her, but it

wouldn't do any good. Without setting the truth straight with Nurse Gray, I couldn't assuage Florence's fears, and I had no intention of doing that. Not until I knew what had happened to Catherine—and myself—out on the moors.

AFTERNOON TURNED TO EVENING, and by the time dinner came, I was convinced Camellia had been waiting until the entire family was gathered to tell the news of my snooping. But, yet again, I was surprised.

She didn't speak a word of it.

Honestly, no one spoke much of anything except for Catherine. She filled the evening with plans for her and Charles and Hazel in the coming months. Talk of travelling to London to see Mama and Papa, hiring a gardener to clean up some of the landscaping around the house, and picnics at the little park in town with bread from the nice baker they'd spoken with at church that morning.

Charles went along with all of it, clearly delighted to see his wife so full of energy. I had to admit it was nice, as well. After seeing Catherine exhausted and spent for most of the week, it felt good to see her smiling.

Still, my concerns wouldn't abate.

When everyone was moving into the sitting room for after dinner conversation, which I expected to include more planning from Catherine and the same narrow-eyed stares from Camellia, I excused myself.

"I'm still feeling a bit tired," I said, pressing a hand to the scratch over my eye. The cut had nothing to do with my exhaustion, but I wanted to remind the happy group of what I'd recently been through in hopes of making them more agreeable.

"Of course," Catherine said, walking around the table to lay a hand on my back. "You need rest. Should I send Nurse Gray in to check on you?"

Catherine had been angry with me the day before, but that all seemed to be in the past now. As sisters, it was never uncommon for Catherine and me to scream our hatred in the morning and then be found giggling behind our hands at the dinner table. We could easily forgive one another for slights.

"No, that won't be necessary," I said, gripping the stair railing.

"Are you sure?"

"Alice knows where Nurse Gray's room is if she needs anything," Camellia said, walking from the dining room to the sitting room, but not before flashing a devious look in my direction. It was the closest she'd come to telling my secret, and I hoped it would be the closest she'd ever get.

"Indeed I do," I agreed with a smile. I bid them all goodnight and went to my room.

Once there, I made quick work of swapping my dress and heels for a tan walking skirt, blouse, and coat. On my way out the door, I grabbed the boots I'd worn the other night. They were still caked in mud, so I carried them in my hand down the hallway as silently as I could.

I hadn't had reason to use the servant's stairwell since my arrival, but I was grateful for it as I snuck down the wooden steps and out the back door.

The sun was sinking low in the sky, coloring the

horizon a deep orange, and I realized it was later than I'd hoped. Still, I couldn't postpone.

The Wilds had told me the season was right for ghostly happenings, but tonight was special. Tonight was a full moon.

I didn't know much about these things, but it seemed to me that if there had been strange activity out on the moors two nights ago, there was sure to be more of it tonight. And this time, I would not run away.

I crouched beneath a back window and slid my boots on. Then, I secured a knife I'd taken from the kitchen earlier in the morning to the inside of my leg with a belt. I felt foolish, like a child playing dress up, but I also felt more prepared. I knew that, if it came to it, I would use the knife to save my life. Without hesitation.

The ground was still soggy from the rain two days earlier, but not nearly as sopping as it had been the last time I'd headed out. My boots squelched in the mud, but I wasn't sucked down to my ankles with each step. So, I made faster work of the beginning of the trail than I had the first time, which worked well since I didn't want anyone in the house to see me heading out.

Once I reached the tree outcropping and the fork in the trail, I looked for the carved stone that would mark the easier of the two paths. I wanted to travel the same ground I'd travelled before, hoping to catch whatever figures I'd seen at their work again and, this time, unmask them. The rock was on the far-left trail, and I headed for it at once.

The trees and ground looked much the same at the start, but as I continued down the path, doubts began to creep in.

The trail had been difficult before, but the ground had been slippery and muddy. My boots lost grip easily, making me slide around the trail, and the rocks had been covered in moss that caused me to lose my footing. Now, there was none of that on this path, yet it still felt more difficult.

The inclines were steeper and the drops were more dangerous, and twice I nearly turned my ankle in a large fissure in the ground that I couldn't see because of the setting sun.

I had never been someone inclined to spend time in nature, so I couldn't be certain, but it felt as though I was blazing a new path entirely.

When I turned around to try and find the house to gain my bearings, I couldn't see the roof through the tree-tops as I could before. I couldn't see anything. And because I'd made so many different turns on different paths, without the peak of the roof to guide me like a star, I had no idea which direction to turn to start home again.

Panic began to tighten around my chest like a band, but I breathed deeply, fighting it off.

I wouldn't be lost out here. At worst, I would be outside overnight. The thought did little to actually comfort me, but I pulled my coat tighter around my shoulders and assured myself I was ready for this. Catherine and Charles would notice me missing and come to find me. When they did, the sound of their searching would help me find my way home. Twelve hours wasn't such a very long time.

Even though I wanted to turn back and start looking for home now, I pressed on. Because, up ahead, just over the green tops of the trees, I saw smoke.

More than the trail or what little instinct I may have had, the smoke guided me. It was a faint cloud of white against the ever-darkening sky, but I knew that where there was smoke, there would be fire. And where there was fire, there would be cloaked figures dancing around it.

At least on these moors, anyway.

So, I fought through my fear and panic and desire to flee until the trees began to thin and the ground began to feel familiar again.

The swells of the hills that would be covered in heather come the spring were the same I'd walked up the other night. Just from a different direction.

Even though I should have been terrified that I was growing closer to the smoke and the shadowy horrors I'd encountered before, I was relieved to know that I was in a place I'd been before. All I would need to do was find the other trail head from this wide-open meadow, and perhaps it would lead me back to the house tonight. If I knew where I was, I could find where I'd been.

The thought of home was still fresh in my mind when I crested a hill and saw the red and orange flicker of flames.

Then, every other thought disappeared.

An instinctual fear took over, chilling me to my center and wiping my mind. I dropped down to the ground, smudging wet grass stains across the elbows and front of my coat, and took shallow breaths.

The fire seemed larger tonight than it had before. It licked up to where the leaves began to grow on the birch trees, threatening to burn up the pile of wood in the center and all of the trees around the outer edge, as well.

It seemed dangerously large. So large I wondered if it could ever be put out.

When the first cry rang out, I burrowed my face into the ground, not caring how dirty I became. My first thought was that I'd been seen, and I wanted to hide.

Then, the sound became a chant.

Hum-drum. Hum-drum. Hum-drum.

Slowly, I lifted my head and watched the fire.

At first, there was nothing more than the dancing of the flames, but eventually, my eyes adjusted so I was able to make out the movement of shadows around the outer ring. The same shadows I'd seen before.

They were nimble and quick, kicking legs and flailing arms around the fire the way I imagined cavemen would have done. The movements seemed archaic and savage. Uncivilized in every respect.

The last light of the sun had turned everything a deep blue, but I knew the figures around the fire wouldn't be able to see me when they were so close to the flames. Their vision would be compromised. Everything else to them would be darkness. As long as I was careful not to get inside the fire's ring of light, I'd go unnoticed.

With that small assurance of safety, I raised myself to my elbows and knees and began crawling forward.

Long grass tickled my chin and nose, and I had to fight back the urge to sneeze, but painstakingly, I made my way down the other side of the hill and onto a flat stretch of ground. Only then did I dare to get to my feet and move in a low crouch. My legs burned from the effort, but I kept my eyes trained on the figures dancing around the fire, watching as they grew larger and larger.

The closer I got, the more I realized the figures were

not inhumanly small or large. They were perfectly aver-
age-sized, which was a slight comfort. Though, I would
have preferred they be small as fairies. The closer I got, as
well, the better I could hear their chant and recognize it
as an imperfect chant.

From a distance, the echoes off of the hills and craggy
rocks made the *hum-drum* sound otherworldly. Now,
though, I could hear that there were two voices crying out
into the night, and they didn't always start and stop at the
same time. Occasionally, their chants overlapped with
one another or one stopped chanting long enough to
cough. That, too, was a small comfort. If they had to
cough, it meant they could be weakened. More so, it
meant life. I couldn't be entirely certain, but I didn't think
ghosts felt the urge to cough.

Twigs and leaves cracked and crunched under my
steps, but it hardly mattered. The fire roared with
destruction, popping and sparking so loudly no one
would ever be able to hear me approach.

I moved until I was ten paces away from the circle of
the trees. Yet still, I couldn't see anything definitive about
the people moving around the fire. I couldn't make out
anything beyond the sway of their dark robes and the
way they bled like inky puddles into the dark ground. I
wanted to get closer, but I didn't dare. Not when they'd
possibly attacked my sister and attempted to attack me
the last time I'd gotten close.

As it turned out, I didn't need to.

The consistent chanting had become nothing more
than a background whirr like wind in my ears. I'd grown
accustomed to it. So, when it stopped, my body grew
alert. Everything felt quiet and still, despite the contin-

uous crackling of the fire, and I held my breath lest the shadows hear me.

One of the shadows stopped and threw up their arms. Their voice was low enough that I couldn't make out exactly what they said, but they seemed to be addressing the moon in reverent tones.

Immediately, I could tell the voice was female, and it startled me in its humanness. I didn't know what I'd expected, but it hadn't been that. I hadn't even expected English. Yet, I could detect a familiar accent.

After a moment, the second voice joined in.

This one was also female and recognition began to dawn somewhere in the back of my mind. A faint tickling of memory.

I shook my head against the image forming there of the elderly women I'd sat with over tea, of the women I'd helped jar and preserve apples, donning robes and dancing around an open fire in the middle of the moors. It couldn't be true. I knew the Wilds were strange, but this went beyond. Didn't it? Maybe I believed they could be capable of dancing around an open flame, but did I really think they could hurt my sister? Would hurt me?

It seemed that the Wilds sisters had gone...wild. They'd gone savage on the moors, running around fires, speaking to the moon. Maybe Catherine had stumbled upon their ritual just as I had and for some reason, they'd attacked her.

Though, as the story went, Margaret and Abigail were the people who found Catherine in the marsh. They brought her back to the house.

However, they'd done so as themselves. Surely,

someone would have mentioned it if the women had been dressed in black robes.

So, perhaps, they attacked Catherine in their cloaks, obscuring their identities, and then changed into ordinary clothes before coming back to "find" her. But none of that made sense with what I knew of the women. They were strange, but kind. They were eccentric, but honest. They made no effort to hide their beliefs from me or anyone else, so what shame would they really feel at Catherine discovering them?

Perhaps, it had something to do with Catherine's resemblance to their departed sister. Catherine had told me the sisters believed her to be the reincarnation of Dorothea. Could it have been that in their desire to see their sister at rest, they were overzealous and hurt Catherine?

Possibilities swirled in my mind until I felt dizzy, and I just wanted to get away. I'd learned and seen more than enough for one night, and it was high time I found my way back to the house. I could discuss all of this with Catherine in the morning. Maybe once she realized the robed figures she remembered were humans and not spirits, she'd be more willing to tell the story of her accident the way it had actually happened. Together, we could convince Charles and Camellia and Nurse Gray that Catherine and I were not insane, but rather, our neighbors were.

Or, if not insane, very strange, indeed.

I crawled away from the fire on hands and knees, just the way I'd approached, and made my way back up the hill. The climb up was difficult, but I was determined and made it quickly. Once I'd crested the hill and gone down the other side a good bit, I rose to my feet and began to run.

I did not sprint as I did before, allowing myself to fall into holes and trip over stones, but I crossed the wide-open area quickly to avoid catching the attention of the sisters.

Now that I knew who wore the robes, my fear had abated. If necessary, I could outrun the older women. I just didn't want it to come to that.

Now that I was far enough away from the fire, I could see that the full moon was bright enough to cast my shadow on the ground. It allowed me enough light by which to move safely over the ground, and to pick out an opening in the tree line up ahead.

The woods still closed around me like a coffin, sealing me in, which only encouraged me to keep moving in order to get out faster. It was too dark under the foliage to be able to tell if I recognized the path, but unlike the path I'd taken at the start of the night that had branched off in many different directions, this one seemed to be a continuous trail like the one I'd travelled a few nights before. So, I felt more and more confident with every step that I was moving in the right direction.

Then, just as I'd grown confident and, therefore, less cautious, I tripped over a large branch.

I noticed the limb just a moment before my foot connected with it, but there had been too little time for me to correct or change course. I fell over the thick branch, landing on my knee. Pain radiated up my leg to my hip, and I held my knee and rolled to my back, groaning.

THE IDEA to scream came to me first. If I could scream loud enough and alert someone in the house to my trouble, they'd come and find me. The problem, however, was that I had no idea how far from the Wilds bonfire I currently was. There was every chance that I would alert the old women to my helpless plight before anyone in the house even realized I was missing from my bed.

While I wanted to believe the women wouldn't actually hurt me, I didn't know that for certain.

I tried to straighten my leg, but the moment I did, pain shot up my leg anew, and I pulled it in close to my chest. I squeezed my eyes tight against the tears burning at the backs of my eyes. If I started to cry now, I wasn't sure I'd be able to stop, so it was better to not start at all.

Keeping my leg pressed to my chest, I sat up on my tailbone. My head and vision swam with pain and exhaustion before clearing, but when it did clear, I looked at the branch again.

It was perfectly in the center of the path, as though it had been left there on purpose. In fact, there were drag marks coming from the right side of the trail. Stranger still, one side of the branch was perfectly cut. It wasn't a jagged snap that had occurred naturally, but there were serrated edges left by the blade of a saw.

The branch had been cut and left, but why?

The moment the thought crossed my mind, something solid and heavy connected with the back of my skull. Pain flared in my head like a firework, and then everything went dark.

14

S herborne raced ahead of me down the street, his long legs outpacing mine two to one.

"Wait. Sherborne, slow down," I called, but he didn't listen. He kept moving down the London streets, turning onto small side roads and disappearing before I'd find him again, towering over the short crowd of pedestrians around him.

I couldn't remember how I'd gotten to London or what I was doing chasing after Sherborne, but it was imperative that I find him. I knew that much.

So, even though my legs burned with fatigue and my feet ached from the crushing pace, I lowered my head and pushed on, determined to catch up to him.

I wondered if this had something to do with my letter. Maybe it had reached him too late, and he couldn't forgive me. Or, even worse, I'd misunderstood his original letter and my returned sentiments, however subtle, were more than he had bargained for.

What if he only wanted to be my friend? What if he only wanted to be business partners?

He'd once made it clear he wanted more than that, but that was before I'd rushed away to New York and before I'd left New York to go straight to Yorkshire, all without stopping to see him.

A lot could have changed by then.

"Sherborne, wait!"

The crowd seemed to part at the sound of my voice, and finally, I was gaining ground. With every step, I grew closer to Sherborne. Even though he never turned around at the sound of my voice, all I had to do was reach out a hand to grab him, and...

My fingers were just about to close around his coat when he spun around.

His long face seemed stretched, his chin resting on his chest unnaturally. And his eyes, usually dark, were black glimmering pools, bottomless and empty. He was Sherborne, but...not.

I backed away from him, but his hand reached out and wrapped around my wrist. His fingers had grown long and thin, the nails curved at the ends into talons that dug into my skin.

"Let me go." *I yanked my arm, trying to free myself from his grip.* "Let me go."

"Wake up, and I will." *His voice sounded different, too, like my mind couldn't remember what he was supposed to sound like.*

"Wake up?" *I pulled on my arm again.* "I am awake."

His black eyes beheld me for a moment, and then he threw back his too long face and laughed. The sound grated on my nerves. It wasn't a laugh, but the sound of dry twigs and leaves breaking against my ear drums. It drowned out every other noise until I couldn't even hear my own voice. My mouth was moving, but no sound came out.

Sherborne let go of my arm, and even though I still couldn't hear anything, I turned and tried to run. Before I could take more than two steps, his spindly fingers wrapped around my ankle.

My weight shifted, and I toppled face first onto the ground. My cheek was raw and my jaw hurt, and my mouth was full of dirt. I coughed, and he dropped my foot and walked around my body to check on me.

Then, he grabbed my leg and began to pull.

The ghoulish version of Sherborne dragged me down the street by my ankle, chanting something I could just barely hear over the strange sound of his laughter that was like dead leaves: wake up, wake up, wake up, wake up.

"I am awake!" I shouted back at him, pulling on my leg to try and free it from his hold. "Stop saying that. I am awake!"

Suddenly, the pulling stopped along with the sound of his laughter and his chant. Everything was quiet. Until...

"Are you awake?"

But this time, the voice didn't belong to the strange Sherborne. It sounded familiar...female.

Before I could place it, there was another sharp blow to my head, and the dream was over.

THE FIRST THING I heard was water. Not fresh running water like a stream or creek, but the sound of water splashing. It happened once, twice, and again, like someone was slipping their hands beneath the surface and bringing water to their face. Then, it went quiet.

I wanted to open my eyes, but they felt too heavy. My entire body felt too heavy.

Each of my limbs ached to the bone, and even the thought of turning my head made my brain slosh. My thoughts were beautiful trinkets hidden behind a soaped-over window. I couldn't seem to make them out as clearly as usual. Everything was happening from behind a veil of fog and confusion, and I didn't know where I was or how I'd gotten there.

The sound of the water stopped and the crunching of leaves started.

I recognized the sound from my dream. It was what I'd heard come out of the strange version of Sherborne. But it hadn't been a dream at all. I realized now the sound had been real. It had been reality leaking into my dream, trying to warn me. But about what?

Wake up, Sherborne had said.

Are you awake?, another voice entirely had asked.

My muddied mind clung to that second question. I rolled the memory over in my thoughts again and again, looking for a foothold, for something to grab onto. I recognized it, but why?

I'd heard voices earlier in the night, too.

Shadows dancing around a fire. Old women praying to the moon.

Margaret and Abigail Wilds had been trying to cast spells on the moors, and now I was being hauled through the woods.

Were they doing this? I'd been confident I could outrun the old women, but were they faster than I could even imagine? Made faster by their supernatural connections? Were they dragging me through the moors now?

Are you awake?

I heard the voice again and it didn't sound like the women. I knew their voices from time spent together in their home, and it wasn't either of the Wilds. So, who?

Before my mind could clear enough for me to be sure, my sore body was hefted up by sure hands under my arms. I managed to crack my eyes open, but there was only more darkness.

Then, a splash.

Icy water soaked through my coat instantly, stinging my skin and stealing my breath. I opened my mouth to gasp, but water flooded between my lips and down my throat. I gagged and choked before I realized I needed to get *out*.

It was so dark that I couldn't tell which way was up, but when I kicked my legs, my foot hit something hard. I assumed it to be the bottom. So, I pressed my foot against it and pushed.

I stretched my heavy arms over my head and felt the moment my fingers broke the surface of the water. Cool air turned them icy, and I knew I needed to get back to the house as soon as possible once I got out of this water. It was too cold to be wet and outside.

My knee screamed in pain as I kicked for the surface, but I ignored it and kept going. My head came out of the water, and I sucked in the cold air, filling my lungs with ice.

Everything around me was dark. The light of the full moon couldn't reach wherever I was, so I had to feel blindly for the edge of the water, hoping it would be close. I didn't assume Catherine and Charles had any lakes on their property, so the body of water had to be small. At least, I hoped it would be.

Those hopes proved true when my fingers grabbed onto cold wet mud.

I threw my arms onto the damp ground and tried to lift myself out of the water, but my coat was so heavy, and my legs were going numb from the cold. I could no longer feel anything below my ankles.

Kicking hard, I released my hold on the bank just long enough to shrug my coat off. It had been a gift from Mama and Papa last Christmas, but I trusted they would understand.

Immediately, I felt lighter, freer. My body was still cold and numbing by the second, but a huge weight had been lifted, and when I grabbed onto the bank and fought to pull myself out of the water a second time, I was able to get my upper body onto the shore.

I waited there, catching my breath, resting my cheek against the cool ground.

Somewhere in the back of my mind, something told me to go to sleep. To rest.

Close your eyes, take a rest. You deserve it.

My eyes fluttered closed, but the moment they did, I heard Sherborne Sharp's voice from my dream: *Wake up!*

If I fell asleep, I would die. I would freeze halfway out of this water. Charles would have to chip me from the bank like ice built up around windows in the winter.

If I got myself out of the water, there would be time for sleep later.

So, I pushed through the exhaustion that hung over me like a fog, dug my fingers into the slippery mud, and pulled. I used every bit of my strength to bring one leg out of the water, my sore knee digging into the ground for more purchase, and then the other.

When I was on all fours, I didn't stop. I crawled like a small child away from the water, moving until I was sure I wouldn't slide back beneath the dark waters. Because I knew, if I went into the water a second time, I wouldn't come out again. I wouldn't have the energy.

I was numb up to my knees now, and soon, my entire body would be numb unless I got up. But I couldn't yet. My chest heaved with exertion, and I rolled onto my back and stared up at the crisscrossing of the trees over the dark blue sky. I watched as my labored breaths created small white clouds in front of me, and I was grateful for each and every one of them. Every exhale meant I was still alive. I was still breathing. Still fighting.

Fighting.

The word caught in my thoughts. I'd been so focused for countless minutes—or hours, I wasn't sure—on getting out of the water that I'd forgotten I'd been thrown in there in the first place. Someone had done this to me. On purpose.

Someone had tried to kill me.

Nearby, leaves crunched, and fear cut through my exhaustion like a scalpel. Though I longed for sleep and rest, my body zinged with adrenaline like an electric current.

Are you awake?

I heard the voice in my mind again, and this time, I wasn't remembering it through a haze of unconsciousness. My mind was clear, and my memory was, too.

I'd heard that voice in my sister's home. At the dinner

table and in the sitting room for drinks. I'd heard that same voice cooing lovingly at my niece through her nursery door.

And I heard that voice again, now, when a figure loomed at the far edge of the water, studying me with eyes that glowed in the darkness.

"You're making this too difficult, Alice," Camellia Cresswell said, her soft tone in harsh juxtaposition to the cruel intent of her words. "You're supposed to be dead already."

15

Camellia sighed and shook her head, seeming as disappointed as if she'd miscounted stitches on a scarf she'd been making rather than having failed to properly murder someone.

"Camellia." My voice was hoarse from disuse and the cold, and I tried to clear it, but phlegm caught in my throat, refusing to budge.

"See?" she said, extending an open hand to gesture at me. "You weren't supposed to know it was me. I thought that would be a comfort to you. To not be aware of what was happening. Despite what you may be thinking now, I tried to be kind. Now, everything is ruined."

She spoke with the same clarity she'd always spoken with, but her words were incomprehensible to me. I couldn't seem to connect what she was saying with the cool, rational way she said it.

"Ah well, there isn't anything that can be done about it now except to see it through." Charles' sister clapped her hands together and advanced around the edge of the bog towards me.

I scooted further away from her on my hands and feet, but it was achingly clear I would need to stand up if I wanted to defend myself. If I wanted any chance at all.

The numbness advanced up my legs like frost crawling across a window pane, but I hoped my legs could still hold me even if I could not feel them. I pressed my palms into the cool dirt and stood up.

My body wobbled forward and back, but I braced myself on my half-frozen stubs and lifted my hands to defend myself. "Don't come any closer."

Camellia's blonde hair caught what little light there was, glistening like a halo around her head. Nothing had ever been more ironic. She was a monster. A demon walking amongst us, murderous in the dark of night.

But why?

It didn't make any sense. I knew Camellia and I didn't get along, but this seemed extreme.

"What are you going to do to defend yourself?" Camellia asked with a laugh. "You can barely stand. You could barely stand even before I threw you in the water. Do you really think you can beat me now?"

No, I didn't. Not at all. But that wouldn't stop me from trying.

"Why are you doing this?" I asked.

"Because of that," Camellia said, pointing an accusatory finger at me. Her top lip was pulled back in a sneer. "You refuse to keep your nose out of everyone else's business. My brother didn't want you to come here, but Catherine insisted, and he can't seem to ignore her wishes even when it is what is best for her. So, he allowed her to send for you. He allowed you to roam this house as though you own it. He allowed you to trick his insane wife into thinking she is well again, when we both know she is as mad as ever."

"It seems to me you aren't qualified to say who is and isn't mad," I said, my hoarse voice managing a touch of sarcasm.

Camellia ignored me and kept talking, her hands fisted at her sides. "Things were fine before you came. We were making things work, but you came and filled Charles' head with lies."

"What lies?"

Her eyes grew large in the darkness, the whites around her irises visible. "You told him I may not be safe around the baby."

So she had overheard my conversation with Charles in his study. Charles had assured me at the time that Camellia would never hurt Hazel. "If you heard that, then surely you heard that Charles had no worries at all. He trusts you with Hazel more than anyone."

"Not more than Catherine," she said, her head turning bitterly towards the trees. I followed her gaze and realized I could see the top of the house from here. It was distant, but visible.

Something like relief flooded my chest, though it was mingled with doubts and apprehension.

Yes, I knew which direction to run now, but that did not change the fact that I could hardly stand as it was. My legs felt numb, my knee was injured, and I didn't have the endurance to outrun Camellia in my current state.

Still, it was a glimmer of hope in what had otherwise been a situation dark as pitch.

"Catherine is Hazel's mother," I said gently. "Of course, Charles trusts her."

Camellia turned back to me with a vengeance, her teeth bared like she was a large cat, wild and starving. "Being a mother doesn't make you deserving. Giving birth to someone doesn't mean you won't hurt them."

"Catherine has never hurt Hazel, though."

"Hasn't she? Hazel nearly died."

"During childbirth," I said with a start. "Catherine nearly died, too. It was an accident, but they both survived."

Camellia was halfway around the bog now, her steps growing larger as she advanced on me. I could see the intention in her eyes. She'd hoped to kill me without me knowing, but my consciousness wouldn't stop her now. She would carry out her plan to the bitter, deadly end.

"Hazel thrived at my breast," she said, pressing a hand to her chest. "She first smiled at me. When she cried in the night, I could comfort her. She wants *me*."

All at once, I understood everything.

"You tried to kill Catherine."

Catherine hadn't seen who'd struck her in the back of the head, and she'd been found half in a bog. Had she crawled out just as I had, but without the energy to make it all the way?

Camellia didn't try to hide her smile. She shrugged. "I nearly did. I would have if those Wilds sisters hadn't found her. Charles wanted to come and look for her, but I assured him she would be back soon. I waited long enough that she should have slipped into the water and drowned. When we did finally go looking, it would appear to be a horrible accident. Something no one could have stopped. But then, we heard the shouts of those elderly witches next door. How two old women could carry a grown woman's body, I'll never know."

Her eyes were glazed, distant as she considered the failings of her first plan. Then, she smiled and turned back to me. "They saved your sister, but no one is coming to save you."

I took another step backward and my back hit a tree. There was nowhere else to go unless I wanted to start running through the trees, and I still didn't feel capable of that. Feeling was slowly leaking back into my feet, but my joints were stiff with chill and my skirt and blouse were crisp and partially frozen around me. It wouldn't take more than a few steps for Camellia to outpace me.

"Think of your own little Grace." I said the words before I could consider their impact, but when I saw Camellia's steps slow, I kept going. "And your husband. What would they think of this, Camellia? What would they say about what you are doing?"

She blinked, dazed like I'd hit her over the head, and then shook her head. "They aren't here."

"Yes, they are," I insisted, pointing to her. "They are with you all the time. You carry them in your heart, and I know they wouldn't want you to hurt anyone. Because hurting me won't change anything. It won't change the fact that Grace is gone. Killing me won't make Hazel your daughter."

Pain contorted Camellia's face into a mask I didn't recognize, and then, before I could think, she was charging at me, hands extended into claws.

My hesitation cost me precious seconds, but I pushed away from the tree and fumbled towards the trail head.

For a moment, I wondered whether I could make it. The path was clear, and if I kept my head and continued moving, maybe I could make it back to the house. I could call out and get someone's attention, and they could save me. It wouldn't have to end this way.

Then, Camellia's hands clamped down on my shoulder.

Her weight crashed into my back, and I screamed, throwing my head back, hurling the sound as far as I could before we slammed into the ground and the breath was knocked from my lungs.

I rolled to one side, tossing Camellia off of me long enough to inhale, but then her weight slammed into me again, shoving my face into the dirt.

I kicked my limbs trying to connect with her, but it felt like fighting a ghost. No matter what I did, I couldn't seem to get a hold on her. But during my fighting, I felt a sharp point in my thigh. That was when I remembered the blade strapped to my leg.

I didn't know how it hadn't fallen off while I was in the water, but it had stayed in place, and now I just needed to get to it.

My arms were pinned underneath my chest, and Camellia was straddling my back, both of her hands slamming my face into the dirt.

"Stay down," she gritted out between attacks. "Stop fighting."

I wouldn't on either account. Never. I would fight her until my very last breath if it came to that.

Finding the energy somewhere inside of myself, I took as deep a breath as was possible and then threw my weight back as hard as I could. It didn't earn me much mobility, but it was enough movement to knock Camellia back for a second and free my arms. And once that was done, I twisted so I was resting painfully on one hip against the cold ground.

Camellia was still straddling my lower body, but I realized she was reaching for something, her arms extended over my head. When I looked up, I saw a rock half-buried in the dirt.

Her weapon.

We were both searching for a weapon, and now, life and death depended on who reached their weapon first. I determined it would be me.

While her weight was shifted forward, I tucked my legs up and reached under my skirts. It was difficult to manipulate the frozen fabric, but I shoved it up until I felt the sopping wet leather straps of the belt around my leg.

I tried to pull the knife free, but the belt was too tight and the blade was too wet. If I wanted it, I would have to undo the buckle first. It wasn't until my fingers were needed for this delicate task that I realized how cold they were. I fussed with the belt buckle, willing my finger joints to loosen and cooperate.

I tried not to focus on Camellia for a moment. Her knee was driving into my stomach while she dug in the dirt to free the rock, but I kept my mind on the task: loosening the knife.

I nearly gasped with relief when the belt unbuckled and the knife slipped free. The blade clattered against the metal buckle and then fell to the dirt. For one agonizing second, I thought I'd lost it in the dirt, but then my hand wrapped around the wooden handle, and I allowed myself to hope.

Just as I brought the knife up, Camellia sat up.

There was only a brief second for me to take in the large rock held above her head and the dirt still falling from it, washing over me like a dirty rain.

There was only a flash of awareness that she planned to bring it down on my head and end my life before I lifted my arm and slashed out at her.

Camellia screamed sharp and strong, louder than I ever could have screamed, and I prayed the wind would be on my side. I prayed someone in the house would hear her and come to find me because, despite it all, I did not want to kill Camellia Cresswell.

She was clearly insane. Heartbroken and lost, and I did not want to be the person who ended her life.

Blood poured from a cut across her nose and cheek, and Camellia dabbed at it with one hand before she gritted her teeth and lifted the rock again. Her arms came down, and I twisted hard to the side, barely dodging the blow.

I felt the impact of the rock in the dirt next to me and, twisted the way I was, I couldn't see where I was aiming when I brought the blade around a second time. But I could feel the grating of bone against the metal.

Camellia gasped and screamed again, but this time, she fell backwards.

I scrambled away from her, rising to sit up so I could see her holding a growing spot of red just above her heart.

"Stop, please," I said, breathless. "No one has to die."

She seemed stunned by her wound, but my words awoke something in her. The coldness I'd seen in her eyes before returned, and she lowered her hands, no longer worried about her wound and how she would explain her cuts and scrapes to everyone inside the house. Camellia didn't seem to care about anything at all except for killing me.

She flipped onto her knees and crawled towards me with malice on her face, her vision so red and murderous she didn't notice when I picked up the rock she'd been wielding only a moment before.

It was only when she was within arm's reach and I began to swing down that Camellia's eyes widened with panic.

Then, the rock connected with her forehead, and her eyes closed.

She fell flat in the dirt with a limp thud and didn't move again.

16

I was still staring at Camellia's limp body in the dirt when I heard footsteps.

Adrenaline still pumping through me, I jumped to my feet and braced myself for another attack, unsure if Camellia had recruited help or not.

I didn't think I had it in me to fight anymore, but whatever was coming for me, I wouldn't meet it lying down.

"Who is it?" I shouted, voice raspy and dry with thirst. "Alice?"

I recognized the voice as Margaret Wilds' immediately. A second later, she walked through the trees to confirm it, Abigail just behind her. When she saw me, her eyes went wide.

"Dear girl, what has happened?" She looked at the rock in my hand and then down at Camellia on the ground. Her brow furrowed. "I assume you had a good reason for attacking her?"

"She tried to kill me," I said flatly. "And nearly succeeded."

This must have been a good enough explanation because Margaret nodded and then walked into the clearing, waving a hand at me. "Put down that rock. No one will hurt you now."

"How can I be sure you won't?"

I knew what strange business they'd been doing tonight, and I knew they'd been doing it much too far away to have heard Camellia's or my screams.

"Because we came to help you," Abigail said sharply, having no patience for my questions. "A cloud covered the full moon during our ritual, and my sister and I both felt a shift in the air. We didn't know what we would find when we got here, but we knew someone was in trouble."

I lowered my arms slightly, the rock resting against my hip. Clearly, the women were not shy about their activities out on the moors. If they were, they wouldn't have admitted them so freely.

Before anyone could say anything else, more footsteps sounded from behind me. I spun around and backed towards the older women, deciding all at once that I trusted them. I had the rock in my hands again when Charles' voice echoed through the trees.

"Camellia?" he called. "Alice?"

I looked down at Camellia lying on the ground, and my voice lodged in my throat. Would Charles be as willing to accept my version of events as the Wilds had? Or would he think I'd instigated the fight and tried to hurt his sister?

"Over here," Margaret called, stepping forward to lay

a hand on my arm. As soon as she did, she flinched. "My goodness, you're freezing."

As though her words broke whatever spell I was under, my teeth began to chatter and my body shivered uncontrollably. Margaret wrapped an arm fully around me, bringing me into what little warmth she could offer.

A moment later, Charles walked into the clearing, as well. Just as Margaret had done, he surveyed the scene—me with the rock and Camellia on the ground. Then, he dropped to his knees next to his sister, cradling her head in his hands.

"What happened to her?"

"Your sister attacked...your sister," Margaret said, realizing the confusion of her words. "Camellia attacked Alice. We came upon them just as Alice managed to over-power her."

"She attacked me and she is the one who attacked Catherine, as well," I said.

Charles blinked, overwhelmed by the information being hurled at him. "How can you know that?"

"She told me." I wanted to keep talking, but my teeth began to chatter uncontrollably, and all at once, my legs gave out. I crumpled to the ground.

"We have to get her inside," Abigail said. "Both of them."

Charles hefted his sister into his arms, and the elderly women, despite my weak protests, bore my weight between them.

As we walked, I faded in and out of consciousness. My head bobbed on my shoulders and it took every bit of strength in me to keep my arms around the Wilds. But sooner than seemed possible, we made it into the house.

Nurse Gray set to work at once, her thin mouth pursed and determined. She moved from my room to Camellia's and back again several times, telling Margaret and Abigail how best to help tend to both of us until, suddenly, she didn't come to my room anymore.

"Camellia is worse off than you are," Margaret said with a small touch of pride in her voice. "You fought well."

I wanted to join her and be proud of myself, but I just felt ill instead. "Will Camellia make it?"

"I think so," she said. "The wound to her shoulder isn't as deep as it could have been, and you missed her heart. She should survive to frown upon us all another day."

I was relieved, but also, terrified. Camellia was not well. I didn't know if it was grief or jealousy or a deadly mixture of them both, but she had gone mad. She couldn't be allowed to stay in this house any longer. Not with my sister and niece. Not even with Charles. She couldn't be trusted not to hurt someone else or herself.

Concern for my family and myself filled my mind until the exhaustion that had been looming over me since I'd pulled myself from the bog began to creep in at the edges of my vision. Every blink became more difficult. The laborious task of lifting my lids sounded less and less worthwhile, and eventually, I slipped beneath the surface of my fatigue and allowed myself to be carried away.

WHEN I AWOKE, it was to bright light streaming in through the windows and birds chirping nearby. It was morning, but as far as my body was concerned, it was still the middle of the night.

I had never been less excited about the start of a new day. I wanted to bury my face back into my pillow and sleep for a lifetime. Two lifetimes if possible. Exhaustion filled my limbs with a heavy weight.

My head throbbed, my muscles protested at the smallest movement, and the morning light that was meant to be cheerful and calming felt like spotlights in each eye, blinding me.

"Alice?"

The sound of my sister's voice made me open my eyes, and once I saw her, I couldn't close them again.

Catherine was poised at the edge of my bed in the rocking chair that, last I knew, had been in her own room. She had a book in her hands, though it looked like she was still on the first page, and she wore her dressing gown. More worrisome than that, when I looked up into her eyes, they were rimmed with red.

There were swollen bags beneath them and tracks down her cheeks.

Catherine had been crying a great deal, it seemed.

I tried to sit up in bed, but the effort made me wince, and Catherine stood from her chair, setting her book aside, and laid a hand on my shoulder. "Don't, Alice. Stay put."

"Why are you crying?" I asked. My voice was little more than a croak, and Catherine grabbed the water from my nightstand and handed it to me. I took a small sip and repeated the question. "Why are you crying? Is Camellia all right?"

"Yes, yes," she said, waving her hand in the direction of the hallway. "The old wench is fine."

My eyebrows raised, and despite it all, I smiled. "I assume you believe my version of events, then?"

"I should have believed you the moment you arrived," she said, grabbing my hand from where it rested on top of the blankets. Catherine curled her fingers around mine and squeezed. "You were right about everything, Alice, and I'm so sorry I didn't listen. I'm so sorry this happened to you. It is all my—"

A sob broke through her lips, choking out the last word, but I didn't need to hear it to know what she'd intended to say.

"None of it is your fault," I said, squeezing her fingers right back. "Nothing. You had so much going on, Catherine."

"But I asked you to come here and then ignored your help when you offered it. You tried to tell me you believed my story, and I refused to listen."

Clearly, there was nothing I could say to convince Catherine this wasn't her fault, so instead, I opted for distraction.

"You know the night I ran screaming through the moors, fleeing ghosts?" I asked.

Catherine frowned and nodded, wiping a stray tear from her cheek.

"Margaret and Abigail Wilds."

"Really?" she asked. "They were out there in robes dancing around a fire?"

I nodded.

Catherine's blue eyes went wide, and her mouth split into a grin. "Don't tell lies like that, Alice. It isn't right."

I lifted my right hand. "I swear it. I saw those old women dancing around a fire under the full moon."

It felt good to laugh with Catherine—to laugh about anything—even if it was at the expense of the Wilds. I had a feeling they wouldn't mind too much.

Catherine asked questions and laughed until there were tears in her eyes for another reason entirely, and then she leaned forward and pressed a kiss to my forehead.

"I'm so glad you are all right, Alice." She tilted her head down, eyes probing. "You are all right, aren't you?"

"Me?" I asked with a grin. "Believe me, I've been through worse. I'll be just fine. I promise."

I'D BEEN TELLING the truth when I told Catherine I would be just fine. I knew I would be, though *when* I would be was another question entirely.

I'd had nightmares every night. Of the moors and the bog. Of shadows chasing me through the trees. I'd wake up crying and sweating and desperate for the sun to rise.

Physically, I wasn't much better. I'd never been so banged up before.

Nurse Gray told me several days later that she'd had to slide my kneecap back into place, rub color back into my numb toes and legs, and clean and bandage too many cuts and scrapes to count. She told me that any longer out in the woods, and I may have lost toes due to the cold.

Even days later, my body ached. Going down the stairs three days after the attack felt like a physical feat unmatched by the rest of humanity. I expected to see crowds cheering at the bottom of the stairs when I finally made it.

Going up them, however, required a very chivalrous Charles to carry me in his arms. I was embarrassed to need his help, but he assured me he didn't mind.

In typical Charles fashion, he never told me specifically that he was sorry about his sister's behavior, but he showed it in as many ways as he knew how.

He smiled at me when I came into rooms, offered to fetch anything at all that I needed, and swore to me that there would be a room in his house for me anytime I wanted it. Though, this particular house in Yorkshire wouldn't be theirs for much longer.

Catherine no longer believed the house was haunted, but she'd taken some of my criticism of her life to heart and realized that, no matter how badly she'd wanted to want this country life, she was more suited to the hustle and bustle of a city. She missed having neighbors close by and friends she could meet up with for tea or lunch. She missed having visitors and hearing cars outside her window. Most of all, she missed me.

She never explicitly said that last part, but I could tell it well enough from her expression.

"Hazel and I will be in London just a few weeks after you get home," Catherine said, marking things down on a hand drawn calendar she'd made. "Charles will stay behind to ready the house for selling, and then he'll follow. Do you think Mama will help me by making a list of available places nearby?"

"If it means seeing her granddaughter every day, I think Mama will build you a house with her own two hands."

Catherine laughed, but Charles frowned. "Maybe not every day."

"But often," Catherine said, grinning back at him and then at me.

It really was nice to see her smile.

"Of course, part of our time will be spent with Camellia," Catherine added a bit somberly.

Charles nodded in agreement and then quickly lowered his head, focusing on a stack of papers in his lap.

He hadn't said much about his feelings on the matter, but Charles and Catherine had both decided the best place for Camellia would be in a private care facility in London. Someplace where she could be separated from society while she sorted out her emotions and came to understand the depths of her delusions.

I hoped just as much as anyone that she could be saved. She'd left the morning before with two nurses and a large male driver I guessed was more of a personal guard than anything else.

There had been a brief conversation about hiring Nurse Gray to care for Camellia, but Catherine and I each voted against it.

Catherine had explained to me that Nurse Gray had been a nurse for terminal patients for years. She was brought in when the patient's life was nearing its end. That was why she kept such a cool, detached manner with everyone—to protect herself and her own emotions. It was also why she'd administered so many medications.

For years, her job had been to make people comfortable, so when possible, she gave Catherine medication to put her to sleep and ease her turmoil, whether physical or mental.

But just because I understood why Nurse Gray did what she did, didn't mean I agreed with it. We all thought it would be best to thank Nurse Gray for her time and talents and then cut ties with her. And anyway, Nurse Gray left the moment I told her I was well enough to tend to my own wounds. After the revelation of Camellia's mental anguish and crimes, Nurse Gray seemed very eager to leave the house and move on to her next patient.

"I think it will be a good move for us all," Catherine said, bringing me back from my thoughts. She leaned down to scoop Hazel up from the blanket where she'd been playing on the floor. The chubby-cheeked little girl blew a spit bubble at her mother and grinned, making an equally luminous smile spread across Catherine's face. "It will be nice to relax into ordinary life for a while."

I knew what 'ordinary life' meant for Catherine. For her, it meant life as a mother and a wife. Life free of a private nurse and accusations of insanity. For Catherine, it meant going back to life as it had been.

For me, however, I wasn't sure.

For the last year, my life had been anything but normal, and I was beginning to think that abnormality was my new normal.

Could I really see myself settling down with a nice husband? Could I imagine cradling my own child the way Catherine hugged Hazel?

I didn't think so.

And yet, when the questions rose to my mind, a face came with them. The image of a tall man with dark hair and equally dark eyes floated in front of my eyes.

17

A week after the attack, I was able to go for walks again.

I only took them early in the mornings or in the early afternoons. Never in the evenings. Never when it was even close to getting dark. And never in the back of the house.

Instead of walking the trails, I walked the long dirt drive that led from the front of the house to the road. I passed by the Wilds sisters while they tended to their gardens out front and drank tea at their window. Sometimes I stopped to say hello, other times I kept going.

Nurse Gray had told me before she left that movement would help me heal so long as I was taking it easy and not pushing myself. So, every day, I walked a little farther. And I planned to continue the practice when I returned to London in the coming days.

Catherine had sent a letter to Mama and Papa telling them what had happened during my visit, so I wondered whether Mama wouldn't try to bar the doors and windows to keep me inside and safe. I'd begged Catherine to keep it all a secret, but she explained that wouldn't be possible, and I unwillingly agreed. The news would get out that Charles' sister was mentally unwell and the rest of the story would follow.

Then too, the cut across my forehead was fading, but not fast enough for it to be gone by the time I returned. Mama would see it and the other scars I'd earned during my fight, and she would be able to tell if I was lying or not.

Today when I walked past the house where Margaret and Abigail Wilds lived, they were burning dead wood in a heap next to their house. Thankfully, they were not dancing around the flames, though the image from that night rose to my mind entirely unbidden and unwanted.

I wouldn't have minded stopping to say hello, but not with the fire.

I didn't want to admit it to Catherine, but when I was reminded of that night at all, panic gripped me. Usually, I could talk myself down, but it took a few minutes. My body would feel as though I was right back in the fight, as though I needed to fight for my life from enemies all around me even though I knew I wasn't actually in danger.

Margaret lifted her hand and waved, grinning at me, and Abigail nodded in my direction. I smiled at the two women and made a silent promise to sit and have some of their terrible home-brewed tea before I left for London. Then, I turned and headed back for the house.

It was close to lunch, and my appetite was beginning

to return. The exercise certainly helped that. Florence had been making scones with every meal, knowing how much I liked them, and I knew they were in thanks for getting both Camellia and Nurse Gray out of the house. She told me she would make me as many scones as I wanted for as long as I wanted them. It would be easy to keep that promise now that she would be moving to London to continue working for Catherine and Charles.

By the time I was nearing the house, my legs were tired and my stomach growled. My knee ached slightly, which was a sign that I needed to get inside and put it up, probably with a cool compress.

I was so focused on the state of my body that I didn't notice the figure standing at the mouth of the driveway until he cleared his throat.

The sound startled me, and I yelped and jumped to a stop. Then, my mouth fell open.

For several long seconds, I convinced myself I was seeing things. I convinced myself that all of the stress of the last couple weeks had turned my mind to mush. There would be no saving it. Because certainly, Sherborne Sharp could not be standing at the end of my sister's driveway waiting for me.

It made no sense.

And yet...

"Alice." His voice sounded nothing like it had in my terrible nightmare that night on the moors. It wasn't sharp or shrill or overwhelming. My name on his lips was deep and soothing and warm. More comforting than I ever could have imagined.

I blinked and shook my head. "Sherborne?"

He took off his hat and held it against his stomach,

both hands folded over it, and bent his head. "I can't tell whether you are pleased to see me, which is why I'm still standing so far away. I didn't want to intrude on your visit with your sister, but you sent me that letter and then left. Then, you stayed away for so long. Your mother is probably tired of seeing me. Also, yes, I'm sorry, but your mother knows we are friends now. I know she isn't fond of me, and you wanted to keep our friendship secret, but I didn't know where to reach you, and I was going mad—"

"You were?" I asked the question only so he would keep talking.

"Absolutely," he said, smiling at my very subtle encouragement. He took a step towards me, and I took one, as well. Slowly, we both advanced towards one another until we met in the middle. Though, once we were there, neither of us knew what to do. So, Sherborne carried on talking.

"Your mother finally told me where your sister lived so I could write to you, but I didn't know what to say. So, I thought a train ride would give me time to think about it. And then, suddenly, I was arriving at the station and asking someone for directions to your sister's home, and...well, here I am."

"Here you are." I smiled up at him, amazed that he was in front of me and that I was so pleased about it.

I'd known when I sent Sherborne the letter that I liked him. More than a business associate, as I'd once described him, and more than a friend, which he'd described himself as. I liked him in a way I'd never liked anyone before, which meant I didn't have any idea at all how to behave around him.

"Do you want to walk with me?" I asked finally.

He nodded and followed me down the driveway towards Catherine and Charles' home. Then, we turned and headed for the back of the house.

I'd avoided the trails there since the accident, but they didn't seem nearly as daunting with Sherborne at my side. In fact, it seemed silly to be afraid of a piece of land at all.

We walked a short distance from the house until we were at the fork in the trails. Sherborne seemed content to keep on walking, but I reached out and grabbed his hand, stopping him. He turned towards me, his dark eyes tracing over my face. I saw them snag on the cut on my forehead.

"I know better than to ask you directly what happened to your forehead," he said, twisting his lips in mild frustration.

I smiled at the familiar gesture and nodded. "Good."

"I know you are a grown woman, Alice," he continued. "I know you can take care of yourself."

"I can," I said, agreeing with him.

His mouth quirked into an amused smile, and he rolled his eyes. "But—"

"No." I shook my head. "There is no *but*. I can take care of myself."

"But," he said again, grinning openly now. "I've also saved you several times. You take on more than you can handle and without someone there to temper your confidence, you are likely to get yourself killed."

If only he knew what had happened less than a week prior. He'd either be delighted he was right or horrified by my recklessness. Probably both.

"And you think you are the person to temper my confidence?"

He shrugged, the movement surprisingly shy. "I could be. If you want."

Being honest about my feelings had never been my strong suit. I could tell someone a harsh truth when it needed to be told, but I had a hard time revealing my own truths. So, despite the answer ringing out loudly in my heart, my mouth stayed firmly shut.

That was probably for the best because Sherborne, made nervous by my silence, kept talking.

"You are a pain, Alice," he said. "You make life difficult for me."

"In your letter you said I make it interesting."

"They are interchangeable," he said quickly, waving away my interruption. "But despite how much trouble looking out for your safety has brought me, I've decided that you are worth every single bit of it."

Emotion crawled up the back of my throat, making it hard to swallow, and my eyes went misty. I blinked rapidly to clear my vision. "I'm delighted to hear I'm worth it."

Sherborne smiled. "Now, are you going to tell me what happened to your forehead?"

I frowned. "Don't you want to hear what I think of you?"

He shook his head, a smug smile on his face. "The blush in your cheeks tells me all I need to know."

I pulled the corners of my mouth into deeper disapproval and swatted his arm. "It seems that if either of us needs someone to temper their confidence, it is you."

"If you're applying for the job, then you are hired."

I smiled up at him, feigning annoyance at his antics, and then quickly felt the mood shift to something less playful. Sherborne's dark eyes captured mine, rooting me to the spot, and I couldn't breath as he took a step towards me. I tipped my head back just as...

"Do you have a visitor, Alice?"

I turned and Charles was standing at the back of the house. He waved at us. "Catherine said she noticed a gentleman walking with you down the driveway."

Sherborne startled and then was his usual casual self an instant later. He bowed slightly at the waist. "I am Sherborne Sharp, a friend of Alice's from London. I am sorry to intrude."

"Never," Charles said. "We'd love to have you for lunch. It's ready now."

Charles walked inside, the back door banging closed behind him, and Sherborne and I both stared after him for a second before looking at one another shyly, silently acknowledging the ruined moment.

"Well, are you hungry?" I asked.

"I am, but didn't you want to go for a walk?" he asked, pointing towards the trail.

I looked into the dark mouth of the trail, imagining the sprawling land beyond. Suddenly, I realized that I wasn't afraid anymore. Not only because Sherborne was now with me, but because the moors were not the place where I'd nearly died.

They were the place where I'd survived.

Fighting for my life amid the barren landscape had helped me realize that I was stronger than I ever knew, and now I would carry that strength with me to London and anywhere I decided to go after that.

Alone or with someone by my side, I knew I could handle whatever challenges came my way next.

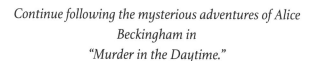

Continue following the mysterious adventures of Alice Beckingham in
"Murder in the Daytime."

ABOUT THE AUTHOR

Blythe Baker is the lead writer behind several popular historical and paranormal mystery series. When Blythe isn't buried under clues, suspects, and motives, she's acting as chauffeur to her children and head groomer to her household of beloved pets. She enjoys walking her dog, lounging in her backyard hammock, and fiddling with graphic design. She also likes binge-watching mystery shows on TV.

To learn more about Blythe, visit her website and sign up for her newsletter at www.blythebaker.com